ON THE PROWL

KATE RUDOLPH

 Created with Vellum

Sparks fly when an ex-military werewolf show up to protect his rock star mate.

When a strange monster threatens Em's rock tour she needs help. But when her sister sends dark and mysterious Andre to protect her, Em is sure she'd be better off on her own.

He's too attractive for his own good, but just because her body wants him doesn't mean she'll let him have her heart.

As the ghostly monster escalates the attacks, Em can't keep going without Andre's help. But the beast may be too powerful even for a werewolf. How can Andre fight a monster that disappears out of thin air?

Finding a way to fight a monster made of magic? Easy.

Convincing a stubborn rock star that he's her fated mate? Andre will need to figure it out before malicious magic tears them apart.

ANDRE'S FUR was soaked through and his paws covered in mud. The scent of rain drenched the air, hiding the precious prey he knew bounded through the forest all around him. The pack sprinted through the muck like it was nothing. Rowe bumped into Jackson, covering her with even more mud. Hunter trailed after Vega.

And Stasia and Owen might as well have been running in their own little pack.

Gibson led them all, and Andre should have felt the pull of family. The rightness of their bond was what kept them all together after the mysterious way they'd all become wolves. But tonight, Andre didn't feel it.

He just felt cold and muddy and he wanted to curl up somewhere warm and sleep.

He must not have been alone. Gibson's farm property spread over acres of Pennsylvania wilderness and they could run for miles without risk of anyone seeing them. But the lights of the farmhouse were in sight through the dense trees, and first Hunter, and then Rowe and Jackson peeled off and headed for shelter.

Andre didn't follow immediately. He didn't want to look too eager, though it was something he'd never admit out loud. He was a goddamned werewolf.

Werewolves didn't cower from a bit of bad weather.

But he'd done his time in the Army and had experienced all the drudgery that went with that. He didn't care if he wore human skin or wolf fur, he just wanted to be *clean* and *dry*. Preferably in a comfortable bed.

Whatever sense it was that held him back finally released him, and he padded towards the house, mud squelching beneath his paws. Andre ran faster, letting his muscles bunch in ways no human body could ever contort.

Maybe the rain wasn't so bad.

The run was cut short when he made it to the covered patio behind the farm. He shook himself off as best he could, trying not to think about how he must have resembled his childhood dog, and stepped towards the sliding glass door.

Before he could step inside, Erin Jackson blocked his path, one human hand held in front of her, the other holding closed the robe she'd slipped on after shifting back to human. "The major will kill you if you get mud on his floors."

Andre huffed out a sound that was *not* a whine, but he backed away from the door and took a deep breath before letting the shift take him. The wolf melted away and he stood up as a man. Even better, most of the mud was gone.

He was naked, but Jackson didn't give him a second look. She only had eyes for one man, not that anyone in the pack would be stupid enough to say *that* out loud. Once inside the house, he grabbed his robe and pulled it on. He could still feel the mud between his toes, but it was a phantom sensation.

"Hunter's gone to get food," Jackson said, picking up her beer bottle and taking a swig before placing it back down on its coaster.

Andre's stomach rumbled at that. Good. He could eat. Sometimes they hunted prey as wolves and there was no need for pizza afterwards. Tonight was not one of those nights.

"Shower free?" he asked. The house was big, but old enough that it only had two bathrooms, one of which was attached to Gibson's bedroom. No one was brave enough to use that one without his permission. Which left six adults sharing a single bathroom. It was a good thing stays at the farm were usually short.

"I don't hear water running." Jackson settled into her seat and left him to discover for himself.

No one was in the bathroom, thankfully, but Andre didn't take his time under the hot stream. He'd been cursed with cold water enough times in his life that he didn't want to inflict it on other people.

Once all the imagined dirt was washed away, Andre headed upstairs, where he could already smell the tangy tomato sauce and cheese of the pizzas Hunter had picked up. It had become a tradition over the last few years. They ran in the woods and when they didn't catch their prey, they ended the night with stacks of pizza.

A feminine laugh burst up the stairs before abruptly being cut off by a moan. Sometimes Andre cursed the slightly heightened senses that came with wolfiness.

He didn't begrudge his friend his mate. Owen's discovery of Dr. Stasia Nichols had led to them discovering more about themselves and their wolfish state in a matter of weeks than they had in the entire two years prior to her coming into their lives. And Owen, who had always been gregarious, was truly happy in a way that Andre hadn't known a person could be.

But he was so damn chipper about it that

sometimes Andre wanted to slug that contented look off his face.

It wasn't a fair thing to think about his best friend, and he'd never dare say it out loud. But he couldn't help thinking it.

"I'm thinking we don't need to save any pizza for them," Leland Rowe said with a grin, bumping his shoulder into Andre's.

"They can eat it cold." There was always more than enough food. Werewolves ate like ravenous beasts, but Hunter had a knack for always getting enough. Then he took another look at Rowe, who was wearing tight jeans and a decent shirt. "You going somewhere?"

Rowe grinned. "I'm checking out this new bar in town. You're welcome to join me. Lots of lonely ladies this far out in the country. And the alcohol is cheap."

Both were true, but Andre wanted a soft bed more than a soft pair of thighs at the moment. Rowe always seemed to be looking for a party when he wasn't on duty. "Have fun."

"Call if you're too drunk to drive," Jackson added. She'd come up from downstairs while Andre was in the shower and was now dishing up pizza for herself.

Rowe rolled his eyes. "Even with the cheap liquor out here I don't have enough cash to be wasted for long. Stupid werewolf magic," he scowled.

"Remind me you said that next time you heal a stab wound," Andre said. They could heal just about anything, as long as it wasn't silver. And luckily, silver weapons were few and far between.

Rowe made a dismissive sound, grabbed a slice of pizza, and headed out the front door.

Andre grabbed food of his own and sat at the counter beside Hunter and Jackson.

"Should we be worried about him?" Jackson asked. She looked at the door for a long minute before digging back in to her food.

Hunter didn't say anything. She was always quiet.

Andre shrugged. "He's a big boy. He can take care of himself."

"You didn't see how much puke he managed to spew on the floor of the truck." Jackson shuddered.

"You didn't clean it up, did you?" Jackson was a stickler for the rules, but even she couldn't go that far. Right?

"I don't clean." Her tone was icy, and Andre filed that information away. He didn't want to get on her bad side.

That was good, at least. Rowe could make his own messes, but he needed to clean them up as well.

Gibson and Vega came upstairs a few minutes

later. Jackson handed Gibson a plate heaping with pizza, which he took with a smile.

"Where's my plate?" Vega asked, eyeing Jackson and Hunter hopefully.

Hunter grunted. "Make your own."

Vega's shoulders sagged, but he did as she said.

This was his family, Andre supposed. For better or worse. And on a night like this, he was inclined to think of them as *better*.

"Have you heard how Mercy's tour is going?" Jackson asked with deceptive casualness. Mercy was better known as Emerald Selby, Stasia's younger sister and one of the biggest rock stars on the planet.

Something jolted low in Andre's gut. No, not his gut. Even lower.

But his cock was *not* going to pay attention to that… *woman*. They'd clashed when they'd met a few weeks ago, and he didn't have any desire for a repeat.

No matter what his cock said.

"Stasia hasn't said anything," he replied gruffly. "Why, did you want tickets?" It came out sharper than necessary.

Jackson blushed and sank down a bit on her bench. "I'd buy tickets if I wanted them."

The major heard their interaction and glared at Andre. "Did something crawl up your ass?" Gibson demanded.

"No, major." But Andre scooped up his plate and

headed for the bedroom he was sharing with Vega and Rowe.

He didn't want to talk about spoiled rock stars who made his dick hard. He had enough to deal with these days.

2

EM WAS the kind of tired that only happened when she went on tour. Bone deep exhaustion made all of her limbs heavy, and the strenuous workout that was every performance made her muscles ache. She was only a few weeks into this US tour and her body hadn't yet adjusted. Give it another week and she'd be fine.

She hoped.

But she couldn't help the nagging sensation that there was something off about this tour. Something didn't feel right.

Or maybe it was her. Em was hiding out in a closet hoping to snag five minutes of privacy before someone came searching for her so that they could shepherd her to her next task. Sound check, she was pretty sure.

At least she had five whole days in the city, even if three days were already gone. She wasn't actually sure *what* city it was. Little details like that fell by the wayside when she bounced from place to place on a daily basis.

Touring had seemed glamorous when she was a young star. It was a way to experience the kind of life she never imagined she could have.

No, that was a lie. She was a Selby. She could have any kind of life she wanted. Jet setting didn't need to come attached to a grueling schedule.

But this was the life she'd chosen.

Em groaned and leaned back against the wall. She was nestled in beside several shelves which were stacked high with cleaning products. If one of the reporters following the tour spotted her in here, they would probably think she was getting high and have the story up online in the hour. It wouldn't get far before her publicist had the counter narrative ready to go. That kind of life had never really been her MO.

But she didn't want the rumors. With the new album just out and not doing as well as expected, she couldn't afford bad press, no matter how good her publicist. Though her record label would probably say that any press was good press.

She had a hell of a story for them. How would they take it if she told them that her sister was a werewolf?

The thought startled a laugh out of her. Yeah, she wasn't going to be telling anybody about Stasia's new condition. *That* would definitely have people thinking she was on drugs.

If Em wasn't in her dressing room, she might have to face annoying questions. She was supposed to be in charge. That was what everybody thought when they thought of a rock star on tour. But Melinda and her army of very efficient assistants had way more say in what was going on than Em did.

She pressed her ear against the door and listened carefully for a moment. But the door was thick and she couldn't hear anything. Rather than wait any longer, Em slipped out of the closet and headed toward her dressing room.

She was thankful that they were staying in the hotel that was connected to the convention center where she was performing. It meant that fans were swarming the place, but at least she didn't need to leave the building for anything. It made her feel safer than normal.

Not that she ever really dealt with danger. She had screaming fans, a few obsessed ones, and there was a lot of fanfiction out there. But her security kept her safe, and she'd never felt like the fans were a danger to her.

She was lucky in that regard. She had heard horror stories of some of her friends who appealed to a slightly younger and more rabid audience. But Em had made the decision to be a rock star, not a pop star, and that came with a slightly different fan base.

At least that was what the record company said.

There were dozens of people milling around in the hallways doing their best to get the stage prepared for the concert. They'd had the luxury of letting the stage stay up between shows, which meant everyone was a bit more relaxed than usual. Stopovers like these were sort of like mini vacations. But Em would be expected to do meet and greets and other events when she wasn't busy performing.

She'd chosen this life, she reminded herself. She didn't get to complain.

At least, not out loud. But it was about time to give Stasia a call and let all of her complaints fall on her older sister's ears. Besides, she wanted to hear how werewolf life was going. If she thought being a rock star was special, Stasia had blown her out of the water.

Em slipped into her dressing room. It wouldn't be long before her makeup artists and costume people showed up to get her ready for the night. But Em had three more minutes to herself. She sank into her chair and looked at the table in front of the mirror. At first she didn't know what she was looking at.

It should have been covered with makeup and jewelry and all of the things that she would need to become her alter ego Mercy, the international rock sensation.

But the table was empty. Empty, and covered in deep gouges. Em reached out to touch, her fingers digging deep into the pulp of the wood. This wasn't some decoration. It looked like a wild animal had gotten in and attacked the table.

Werewolf.

The thought whispered in the back of her mind. It would have been crazy if she hadn't just met a pack of them a few weeks before. Her heart rate kicked up and she spun around, eyes darting madly trying to find the threat.

But she was alone in her dressing room.

Was this some kind of prank? Was somebody having fun at her expense? They couldn't know about Stasia. Not about Owen or Andre or Rowe or any of the rest of them. She hadn't said a word. Though maybe one of the assistants or one of the band members had caught her looking up the Wikipedia page to try and learn more about wolves.

No.

One of her costumes was on the ground, and Em bent to pick it up. Shredded. Some of her costumes had artfully gaping holes that let people see her skin or a mesh approximation of her skin tone, but this wasn't anything done by design. She set the top down on the desk, and the rip in the clothing matched the gouges in the desk.

Wicked claws. She could imagine them.

Her hands shook and there was a scream caught in her throat, but she couldn't articulate it. She was too aware of all of the people outside of the dressing room who would come running if she made a noise.

And she couldn't let this information end up in the tabloids.

With shaking hands, she reached for her cell phone and brought up Stasia's number, dialing and praying and hoping that her sister picked up. It took several rings before she did.

"Hey! Are you supposed to be on stage?" Stasia asked, a smile clear in her voice.

"I need your help." Em didn't waste time with small talk. "I think I have a werewolf problem."

3

"SHE'S MY SISTER, I have to go." Stasia paced back and forth in the living room of the farmhouse while the pack watched her move. She cast a helpless glance at her mate, begging for his agreement.

But Owen had an uncharacteristically grim expression on his face. "Stasia…" Whatever he needed to say, he couldn't get the words out.

"You aren't stable enough," Andre said, saving him from delivering the blow himself. He liked Stasia. He really did. She was good for Owen. But she'd only been a werewolf for a bit more than a month, and she didn't quite have control of her shift. Given the likelihood of cameras swarming around Em, they couldn't risk Stasia giving them away. Not only that, Stasia would not want the spotlight on her.

But she was adamant. "I have control. I'm a

doctor. If I *don't* have control, people get killed." Her eyes flashed gold as she made the statement, and her lips pulled back to reveal too sharp teeth.

Andre raised his eyebrows as if that answered that. A little bit of eye shine wouldn't give them away, but it was just the first step. What if her fangs dropped? Or her claws came out? What if she shifted all the way? He didn't say any of it out loud, and he didn't have to. Owen grabbed her hand and stopped her pacing.

"She's my sister. She needs help." Stasia sounded desperate.

"I could go," Bryan Vega piped up from where he sat on the couch in the corner of the room.

"No." The denial came from all of them.

"We don't need another accidental pack member," Leland Rowe said with a glare at the young wolf.

"That was *one* time. And I had been shot," Vega protested, his face a mask of indignation.

"That doesn't change the facts," said Gibson. The major surveyed them, his steely gaze taking all of them in and analyzing what would be best.

"My schedule is free," Rowe offered with a grin.

Andre tamped down the growl in the back of his throat. Rowe was a good bodyguard. Even if he was a party boy. He could do the job just fine. But Andre didn't want him around Em.

And why was that?

He had no claim on the woman. He didn't even like her. She was, at best, a distant acquaintance. He owed her nothing. And he should just be happy that Rowe wanted to go and be done with it.

He was anything but happy.

"I'll do it," Andre spoke before the thought fully entered his mind.

That quieted everyone. Gibson gave him an unreadable look. "That could work," he said cautiously.

"I offered," Rowe challenged with a bristle. He glared at Andre as if Andre had taken away a particularly juicy meal.

"I'm pulling rank." They didn't fall back on their military ranks all that often. Things had gotten so weird after they were drummed out of the military that clinging to old hierarchy didn't make any sense. They were all equals when it came to knowledge about werewolves. Except when it came to Gibson. He didn't necessarily know any more than they did, but he was their commanding officer now. It was hard to ignore a CO even years out of the service.

Of course, pulling rank wouldn't be enough to get Gibson to agree. "I'm not a super fan," Andre said to make his case. "I'm not sure I've ever heard one of Em's songs. I'm not going to get starstruck. I can keep my head on the case." Though the fact that he was campaigning so hard for the job might have said otherwise.

"Can you?" Rowe glared, and Andre had the faint worry they'd end up coming to blows. Why did Rowe want this so bad? "And just because we talked about music doesn't mean that I'm a super fan. Who the hell talks like that?"

Andre knew he was fighting too hard. He didn't normally get excited about things, and he certainly didn't let his desires show. But now that he had offered, he wanted to be the one to go out there and protect Em. There was some kind of supernatural threat and he needed to uncover it and get it away from her. She had already been dragged halfway into this life when her sister was turned into a werewolf right in front of her. They owed it to her to keep her safe.

It didn't matter that she annoyed the shit out of Andre. It didn't matter that they had clashed the one time they'd met.

It didn't matter that he had been three seconds away from kissing her.

He pushed that thought away. It was irrelevant.

He had a job to do.

"What did she tell you?" he turned and asked Stasia. The call between the sisters hadn't been long. And Em had been lucky. Only Jackson and Hunter had left to head back to the city. He, Gibson, Stasia,

Owen, Rowe, and Vega were all still at the farm and ready to discuss the job. They could act quickly.

Some of Stasia's nervous energy melted away as she spoke. "She found something that looked like a werewolf tore it up. She sounded freaked. But then she had to go do sound check. There's a concert tonight."

Andre almost scoffed, but held it back. It sounded like someone had played a little prank and Em was freaked out. "Doesn't she have security of her own?"

She nodded. "Yes. I've met them. They're a good team. But they don't know anything about us." Stasia gave a look around the room. "And it's not like Em will want to reveal the secret. I don't know if it's anything. But she doesn't get hysterical. She's about as level-headed a person as I've ever met."

"Is there such a thing as a level-headed rock star?" Rowe smirked.

Andre wanted to shove him for insulting Em, even though part of him agreed with that statement. It took a special brand of crazy to crave fame.

"That's my sister you're talking about." Stasia glared.

Owen growled. He didn't need to say anything. And the growling was new, ever since he had mated with Stasia. If that was what came from finding a mate, then Andre hoped he never did.

He was a human who'd happened to turn into a

wolf. He didn't need to bring those traits into his human form.

"Sounds simple enough," Andre said, as if it was already decided. "I'll show up, take a look around, and determine whether or not it looks like a prank. And if she has some sort of supernatural foe, then I'll deal with it."

"Do we think other wolves exist?" Vega asked.

"I don't know, but I'm about to find out."

Two years ago, he and his pack had been kidnapped by some sort of evil sorcerer in the woods all while they were stationed in Germany. One ritual later and they were turning into wolves. But Stasia was the first evidence they had that they could *make* other wolves, and they had no idea if other packs existed.

Magic had to exist; Andre had witnessed it with his own eyes, even if he didn't know how common it was or if witches and warlocks were still a thing of legend. But were there other wolves? Or were they an anomaly?

It was time for him to go find Em and find out.

4

EM HAD FREAKED out over nothing. She was sure of it now. She'd gone to sound check and everything had gone off without a hitch. Then she had given one of the best performances of her entire tour.

No werewolves rushed her on the stage. Not even anyone in a werewolf costume. It had been a stupid prank. Probably one of the crew pulled it off. And they had no idea that it had affected her so deeply. How could they? It wasn't like she had told anyone about her sister.

She regretted calling Stasia. She was the stereotypical older sister, at least when it came to Em. And she would want to fix *everything*. She was going to show up at the hotel, take a look around, and try and run Em's life.

It would be torture. So Em was going to need to

head her off at the pass. There was no calling her off at this point, not when she'd been so worried on the call. She was bound to show up soon enough, and Em wanted her gone as soon as possible.

Did that sound that cold-blooded? Probably.

But the tour was her world. And she needed to protect it. Stasia wouldn't understand everything about tour life. Sure, she could control an emergency department in a hospital like no one's business, but this was a different kind of chaos. And Em usually thrived in it.

She'd just finished up her morning rehearsal and had an hour free in her schedule before she had to do a quick media appearance. She scampered back to her dressing room in defiance of the prank from the night before. She was surprised to see a crew member already in the room. The young woman had purple streaks in her hair and wore torn jeans and a T-shirt from a band that had been Em's opening act three tours ago.

The young woman startled when Em walked in. "I'm sorry. Melinda sent me in here to do some organizing. I'm Vi." She offered a faint wave, as if she was scared Em was about to have a diva moment and scream at her until she left.

Melinda Ramsey was the woman in charge of this tour. She kept things running so that Em could give the great performances she needed to. And Melinda had a fleet of crew like Vi who jumped whenever she gave the command.

Em knew that her dressing room wasn't really a private sanctuary. Unless she specifically asked for privacy, people were in and out of it at all times of the day. It was a necessity. They had limited space backstage, and most her costumes were in the back of the dressing room.

The costume crew had to look at them from time to time to repair any damage that occurred during the shows or during travel, and at this venue her dressing room led right back into one of the larger storage closets. It was a matter of practicality that a few of the road crew would need to be in and out during the day.

Anyone could have done the prank. This room was rarely locked. And as she was seeing right now, anyone could come in.

"You're fine," she told Vi. She wasn't about to throw a wrench into the finely honed machine that the tour was supposed to be. "What's Melinda have you doing?"

Vi blew out a breath and her shoulders sagged. "I'm doing another check on your costumes. Melinda thought she heard the costumer complain about a few tears, and she wanted me to make sure that nothing was out of place. We don't want you going on stage naked. No wardrobe malfunctions."

"Right." Vi clearly meant that for a laugh line, but Em didn't have it in her to share the joke right now. Especially not when she was wondering about tears in her costumes. The offending piece of fabric was on the ground right by Vi's feet, and Em wasn't sure if she had seen it yet.

She knew she should probably say something. Call attention to it and get it taken care of. They could repair the costume like nothing had ever happened or replace it if it was beyond repair. Then she could forget about the prank and get on with her life. Of course, there were still the scratches on the table. But with the clarity of morning, they hardly seemed as bad as she'd feared.

But she couldn't get rid of anything before Stasia arrived. Her sister would insist on seeing the costume and the table. It was stupid. But it probably had something to do with spooky werewolf magic. Something that Stasia would insist that Em didn't understand.

Em sank down into her chair and pulled out her phone. It was strange. She had expected Stasia to give her a call to let her know when she would arrive. Instead, Stasia had sent a text saying that she was discussing the issue with everyone and they would talk later.

Em didn't know what that meant. Well. *Everyone* had to mean the werewolf bodyguards that made up

Stasia's pack. But what was there to discuss? It wasn't like this was an official job. It was, at best, a favor. And she didn't need a werewolf bodyguard, not when her sister would do.

She really wished she hadn't said anything.

Stasia would never let her live this down.

"All done," said Vi, standing from where she had been crouched in front of the costumes. "I'll let you have your dressing room back."

"Thank you." Em had just enough time to sneak in a catnap, and she didn't think she'd ever had a better idea. There was a small couch tucked into the back of the room and she headed to it and laid down, not bothering to cover herself with a blanket. The door opened and closed and she was sure that Vi was gone.

And then it opened again. Em didn't bother to open her eyes. "Did Melinda want something else?" she asked Vi.

"Who's Melinda?" asked a male voice that she recognized.

That wasn't Stasia.

What was Andre doing here?

5

THE STRANGE SCENT of the purple-haired crew member teased Andre's nose until he caught sight of Em. She wasn't just as he remembered her. A month ago, she had been stretched to the breaking point by the knowledge that werewolves existed and worried that her sister might die.

Today she was still tired. He could see the beginning of bags forming under her bright blue eyes, but that was mostly due to her incredibly pale skin. Her long blonde hair fell in waves past her shoulders, and she wore a dark tank top and tight black pants. Was that business casual for a rock star? Just looking at her made Andre's body come alive, but he had to push that thought away.

"Who is Melinda?" he repeated. There were a dozen or more scents swirling around the dressing room, and he assumed one must belong to the Melinda person. He'd passed by far more people than he'd expected to to get to Em's room. It took a lot to keep a music tour running.

Em was looking at him like he'd grown two heads. She looked over his shoulder at the door and blinked hard, as if she could magically make him disappear if she thought about it hard enough.

Andre wasn't going anywhere.

"I called Stasia. What are *you* doing here?" she demanded, arms crossing under her breasts and pushing up enough cleavage that he had to force himself to look away.

What the fuck was going on?

Those kind of thoughts were the opposite of professional, and Andre prided himself on his professionalism. He wasn't going to think with his dick. He was here to make Em feel better and get to the bottom of whatever was plaguing her. He had planned for this to be a simple trip.

Show up, figure out if there really was a threat. Probably figure out that there was no threat at all. And then go on his way. Easy peasy.

But Em's so-called security hadn't flagged him as he walked into the building. No one had stopped him, and he had made no particular effort to sneak in. He didn't like that just about anyone could get inside and find her. Even if there was no supernatural threat, he was going to take care of *that*.

"You know Stasia couldn't come. She's still dealing with… you know." They seemed to be alone enough in her dressing room, but that crew member had just come out, and he wasn't going to risk talking about supernatural business where anyone not in the know might hear.

"I thought she was doing fine." Em's face scrunched up and Andre refused to find it cute.

She was a beautiful woman and she knew it. She was a rock star. Beauty went with the territory. And he couldn't let himself get distracted. When he spoke, it was more gruff than necessary, but he couldn't afford to get too friendly. "There's no need to risk her losing control. But she's okay." He didn't know why he had the need to comfort Em, to assure her that everything really was okay. But his wolf nudged at the edge of his consciousness and wanted him to make her feel better.

Andre wanted his wolf to shut the hell up. It went haywire whenever he was around Em, and he was beginning to see how much of a mistake it might have been to come here.

"I freaked out," said Em. She was a mix of business and apology, apparently accepting that Stasia wasn't coming. "I think it was just a prank. Everything's fine. You can go back home and tell them you checked in and we'll just pretend this never happened. Okay?" She offered him a winning smile.

That kind of smile might have worked at award shows and on magazine covers, but it didn't work on him. And even though he had been thinking right along those lines, he wasn't going to give in to the temptation of doing a shoddy job. "You called for a reason. At least let me check it out." He didn't want Gibson, or worse, Stasia, to ream him out for shirking his duty.

Em's shoulders slumped, and Andre had to curl his hands into fists to keep from reaching out and offering her comfort.

Had his body been possessed by some sort of hormonal monster? What was going on?

This was a job and he had to do it. He didn't need to *comfort* Em. And attraction? Out of the question.

Em bent down and scooped up a pile of black fabric before unceremoniously throwing it at him. "This is what freaked me out. This and the table." She ran her hand briefly over its surface. "It's stupid. Just take a look, agree with me, and leave." She gave the order like a woman used to being obeyed.

But Andre was out of the military, and he didn't have to follow orders anymore. Especially not from spoiled rock stars. If she hadn't made it a command, he might have just given the garment a quick look and dismissed it. But an evil part that lived deep inside of him wanted to annoy her. So Andre took his time, laying the outfit out on the floor and examining every inch of it.

First with his eyes, then with his fingers, and then, embarrassingly, with his nose. It still felt strange after all these years to use his wolf senses in his human form. They weren't super heightened. He couldn't differentiate between every human scent he came across when he wore his human skin. But he could sense more than he remembered sensing when he had just been a normal man.

"This doesn't smell like anything." He spoke more to himself than to Em, trying to figure out why the garment in his hands confused him so much.

"What?" Em's voice was laced with confusion.

Andre picked up the outfit and buried his face in it. He caught a hint of Em's scent and something almost familiar. Another hint of that crew member who had passed him in the hall. But it was barely a trace. Other than that, there was *nothing*.

And that made no sense. These clothes would have been handled by a handful of people, and there should have been a trace of detergent or the water it was washed in or dry cleaning chemicals. But there was nothing.

If Andre closed his eyes and ignored Em and the crew member's scent, it was like there was nothing in front of him.

But he could feel the fabric in his hands.

Weird.

Weird and not a prank.

"It doesn't smell like anything," he repeated, surer this time, even if it made no sense.

"We do clean things around here," Em pointed out. She sank down onto the couch she had been laying on and glared at him. "Someone probably just Febreezed it or something. They tried to cover their tracks. It's nothing." But she didn't sound as confident as she would have if she really believed that.

"Febreeze has a scent," Andre had to point out. "And I don't mean that this thing doesn't smell like detergent or Febreeze, I mean it doesn't smell *at all*. It's like it doesn't exist. Do you understand?" He needed her to get this. He wasn't speaking like he was a man. He was speaking like a werewolf.

For a second he thought she would trust him. Then she shook her head. "I'm sure it's fine. So it smells a little weird. Things smell weird. Does it smell like a werewolf?"

"I can't say that werewolves have a particular smell." He only knew his own pack, and they just smelled like themselves.

That seemed to mollify her for some reason. "Okay. You did your job. You confirmed that it's not a shifter. So you can go report back that everything is safe and we can pretend that we don't know each other and we never have to see each other again. Good?" She offered him her fakest smile and pointed towards the door.

Andre let the clothing drop to the ground and stalked towards Em, towering over her and getting right into her space. It should have been frightening. He knew what fear smelled like, and he expected the scent to start emanating out of her. But that's not what happened. Something heady and hot tickled his nose.

Not fear at all.

And his body responded. He wanted to lean in and feel her soft skin against his. It wouldn't take much. What would she taste like?

He needed to know. His wolf demanded it.

And he refused to give in. This wasn't rational.

Andre tore himself away and backed up several steps. "I got here without being questioned by your security. If someone did this, they could get to you."

Em shuddered. A door slammed down the hall, and she sprang up off the couch. "We shouldn't be talking about this here. Follow me."

He did. She led him down a maze of halls and over a little bridge that connected the convention center to the hotel. They got in an elevator that required a room key to use it and went up to the top floor.

"I don't want us arguing where anyone can hear it. God knows what will happen if the W word gets out there." She shook her head and offered him a wry smile.

He wanted to smile back. And he didn't want to argue. Em needed a bit more muscle, and he was willing to give it. He just had to make her see that. "Just let me stick around for a couple of days. I'll make sure nothing weird is going on. You know Stasia would want that." Andre wanted to think that it was a point of professional pride that was pushing him to stay with Em, but he feared it was his wolf's lurking desires that had him trying so hard.

He didn't even *like* the woman. She set his hair on end.

And yet he couldn't stay away.

She groaned as he played the sister card. But it was true. Stasia would use all of her brand-new werewolf mojo to punish him if he let her sister get hurt.

Em's eyes were pleading, as if *that* would make him relent. "Everything's fine. And I don't really want the tabloids noticing some new hot guy hanging around me with no purpose."

"Hot guy?" He thought she was hot? Good to know. His wolf preened at the thought, and he started to imagine just what *else* they could do together in the name of safety.

Em opened her hotel room door and let him inside, pointedly ignoring his remark. Once the door closed behind him, she turned and crossed her arms. "Okay. Say your piece."

But Andre didn't say anything at first. Her room had that same lack of scent that he hadn't smelled on the garment. He walked further in and looked at the king-size bed that dominated the center of the room. The sheets were all torn up, as if someone had taken claws to them. And just like with the outfit in her dressing room, there was no smell at all.

He was grim as he spoke. "I think I rest my case. You need me."

6

Everything had been fine in her room that morning. Em was sure of it. She walked around Andre, ignoring his comment, and got close to her bed.

The sheets and pillows were all torn up. It looked like a wild animal had gone on a rampage. A wild animal? Or a werewolf? Her hands began to shake as she pulled one sheet back and saw that the damage hadn't gone all the way to the mattress. Thank God. That would be difficult to explain.

A hollow laugh escaped her throat. It wasn't like the rest of this would be *easy* to explain. Who would do such a thing? And why?

She didn't have anything to do with werewolves or magic or any of that bullshit. That was Stasia's realm. And if there was a werewolf in her room right now, she would give them a piece of her mind.

Wait. There was a werewolf in her room.

She spun around and glared at Andre, as if he were the one responsible for all of this.

He had no right to be so fucking attractive. Seriously. Cropped light brown hair that was longer on the top and styled in a way that he would never admit to taking time doing, but she knew enough performers to know that he didn't roll out of bed like that. Piercing blue eyes and strong cheekbones. And she was sure his tight T-shirt was hiding muscles on muscles. And it wasn't hiding them particularly well.

He was the kind of guy that made a woman feel safe and a little reckless. Like he could protect her from anything except from himself.

But Em didn't do bad boys: that road led to heartbreak. She didn't do dark and dangerous. And she certainly didn't do werewolves.

Andre had disliked her from the moment he saw her for no reason other than the fact that she... existed? They hadn't even spoken before he started glaring.

And she did not have any patience for his crap.

Rather than start another argument, she whirled back around and started looking around her bedside tables and all the other areas in the suite where she had put her things.

"What are you doing?" Andre demanded. "You're getting your scent on everything."

Stupid werewolf bullshit. "I'm looking to see if anything was stolen."

She didn't carry much in the way of valuables with her on tour, not personal valuables anyway. She had a phone which she kept with her most of the time or put in the hands of a trusted member of the crew, and she had a computer that was either kept in her safe or in her dressing room.

She opened the safe and saw that her computer was still there and her phone was in her pocket. The only thing left to steal in her room were her clothes, and from what she could see, nothing had been taken. She told Andre as much.

"You thought this destruction was a cover for petty theft?" Skepticism dripped in each of his words.

Her jaw clenched and she curled her hands into fists, but kept them at her side. "Do you think I'm an idiot? Because you're talking to me like I am one." It was easier to be angry than to be scared. Because if she let that anger melt away, she was going to be fucking terrified. Someone or *something* had come into her room and assaulted her bed.

What if it had come in when she had slept?

She made a noise and buried her face in her hands at the thought. Someone could have watched her sleep, could have attacked her and torn her open with terrifying claws like it was nothing. And her security wouldn't have ever known.

She didn't cry. There were no tears. But her breath came fast and she realized she was hyperventilating.

Then Andre was there, one hand on her back rubbing up and down in a soothing motion.

For a moment it felt good. For a moment she let herself be comforted. And then she tore away and put space between them.

"Is this another werewolf?" she demanded.

There was a contemplative look on Andre's face. "I don't know."

"Are there other werewolves?" She had heard the story about how Andre and his pack had been turned into werewolves. It strained credulity. Evil wizards. An ancient forest. Kidnapping. The US government discharging a bunch of soldiers to avoid an international incident. She didn't know which part was the hardest to believe. "If you don't know, then what good are you to me?"

There was that anger again. She let it sizzle in her veins. Yes. She wanted this anger. She wanted anything that would stop the thoughts of what some rampaging werewolf could do to her if it got into her room when she was all alone and unprotected.

Andre's eyes flashed that golden glow of his wolfy side and he stalked towards her, towering over her in a way that should have been intimidating. She caught a hint of his scent, something dark and masculine that she wanted to rub all over herself.

No, it wasn't his scent that she wanted rubbing all over her. It was him. Fear and desire swirled around inside of her, warring for dominance. She wasn't afraid of Andre. No matter how frustrated she was with him, she knew he would never hurt her. At least not on purpose. He had come here to protect her. But why did it have to be him? Any other werewolf would've been better. She had gotten along with the rest of them well enough.

Okay, maybe not Vega. She didn't need anyone else accidentally getting bitten.

"You need me, sweetheart." He got in close. She wouldn't have to lean in very far if she wanted to kiss him.

Which she was not going to do. Both because she didn't like him and because now was not the time. But holy hell did this guy push all of her buttons.

"Don't call me sweetheart," she scowled even as something deep, *deep* inside of her warmed at the term.

"Honeybun, darling, sweetie." Somehow he made those words sound sinister. "I'm the only one standing between you and an angry clawed beast. Are you really going to send me away?"

She wanted to. It would be stupid. Probably suicidal. Because while she could pretend that the incident in her dressing room was a prank, what had been done to her sheets here wasn't. The dressing room wasn't private. But her hotel room was supposed to be. It was the closest thing she had to a sanctuary.

And someone had come and violated that.

Their gazes locked. He was determined to stay and she wanted to send him away. And they both knew that he had already won this fight. She wasn't stupid. Something was going on that her regular security couldn't handle.

Something was going on that required a werewolf's protection. And the only werewolf she had at her disposal was Andre Gordon.

Stupid, hot, infuriating Andre Gordon.

If he didn't take a step back, she was going to do something to him. Probably kiss him. Maybe punch him. Maybe both?

She didn't know where these violent tendencies were coming from. The air was thick with possibility and they needed to do something to break it.

Andre reached out, and his fingers brushed her arm. She had no idea what he was planning. And before he could do anything, she heard someone slide a key into the lock and open the door.

Andre whirled around with a growl.

Andre's growl turned into a snarl as a dark-haired woman with broad shoulders walked into the room. She looked at him standing in front of Em, his body protecting hers, and reached for something on her belt. He was ready to launch himself at her. Was she the one who was scaring Em? Why did she have a key to her room?

"It's okay, Darlene. He's a friend. Sort of," Em called from over his shoulders.

Andre wanted to look back at her and ask what that was supposed to mean. But between the protective instinct driving him, the lust coursing through his veins, and his need to solve the puzzle of what was trying to hurt her, he didn't have much energy left to parse that sentence.

Em tapped on his hip to move him to the side,

and he found himself moving without even thinking about it. They needed to have a talk about who was calling the shots when it came to keeping her safe, but clearly Em didn't fear this woman and so Andre would follow her lead.

For now.

Em stepped between them and did the introductions, gesturing between them as if they were meeting at a party and not in her hotel room after some kind of creature had attacked. "Darlene, this is Andre. Andre, this is Darlene, my head of security."

"And you snuck him into your room why?" Darlene asked calmly. There wasn't an accusation in the question. If she was the head of security, it was her job to know who was around Em and what they were doing at all times. Of course, Darlene and her people hadn't noticed Andre at all so far. So he seriously doubted her skills.

"He's a private investigator," Em explained with a smile.

Since when? But Andre was interested to see where she was taking this.

She continued as if she wasn't spewing lies. "I called him in because of the weird shit that's been happening the past couple days. I just wanted him to take a look."

"There's been more weird shit?" Darlene asked,

arms crossing. Yeah, that body language wasn't good, and Andre didn't need to be a real private investigator to know it.

Em nodded her head towards the bed. "When we got in here, these were all torn up."

Darlene took a few steps into the room, and Andre wanted to stop her from getting any closer. He had a good whiff of her scent, clean and a bit fruity from whatever soap she was using, and it definitely didn't smell anything like the lack of scent that came from the sheets or the costume.

"You didn't see who came in?" Darlene asked, eyes raking over the destruction and expression growing darker by the moment.

"Did you?" He couldn't help himself from asking. She was supposed to be the one doing security.

Darlene glared at him. Well. He wasn't making a friend there. Somehow he would learn to live with that.

"I'll have housekeeping come up and take care of it and inform the rest of the team that we need to do more patrols," said Darlene with a decisive nod. "Is an hour enough time for you to look around? Em needs to be back in the convention center soon."

An hour was nothing. But Andre didn't know what he was looking for. He would probably need to pull out his phone and search for tips on how to be a private investigator on the Internet, but he wasn't about to tell Darlene that. "I can make it work," he promised.

She nodded, her tight expression loosening a bit when he didn't fight her. "I'll let you two *investigate*." And there was a heavy hint of suspicion in that word. Darlene left them alone in the room, the door clicking shut behind her.

"She thinks we're fucking, doesn't she?" he asked Em. And his cock perked up at that thought.

She shrugged. "Probably."

Score one for the private investigator. Speaking of. "Why did you lie to her? I'm not a PI." For some reason, some people thought they were the same thing. Andre's job was to jump in front of bullets, not figure out why they were being fired.

Em threw her hands up in the air. "What was I supposed to do? She's my head of security. I don't want her to feel like shit because of supernatural crap that she could not possibly anticipate. Her job is to keep crazy fans and paparazzi away from me. It doesn't involve protecting me from werewolves."

Andre could see her point, and for the first time he had a bit of pity for the head of security. Maybe it wasn't her fault that he had gotten through. He wasn't a crazed fan and he certainly wasn't paparazzi. "Do you need to go back to the stage?"

Em shook her head. "I still have some free time before Melinda comes looking for me."

"Melinda?" He would probably need to make notes of all of these names. And that was something he was used to doing. He wasn't a PI, but he was a bodyguard, and keeping track of all of the people his client interacted with was just part of the job.

"She runs the show," said Em with an exasperated smile. "She's got schedules on top of schedules on top of schedules, and if we don't follow them, smoke comes out of her ears and she gets really angry and then she yells and I don't like it."

That startled a chuckle out of him. "I've had COs like that before."

They shared a smile, and this time it wasn't angry or heated or anything except a little bit of camaraderie. And that was scarier than anything else.

Andre tore his gaze away from her. "We don't have much time. Let me take a look around."

The hotel room was huge. There was the main bedroom with the king bed dominating the space. There was a bathroom that was bigger than the apartment he used to share with Owen. And a part of him was tempted to fill up the tub with hot water and just soak in it, it looked so comfortable.

There was a living room area with a large couch and a TV large enough that it would appear that he was on the 50-yard line of any football game he watched. And there was a kitchenette with a miniature fridge and a small stovetop and a microwave. It was more of an apartment than a hotel room.

Andre left the bed for last, stalking through the room and searching out anyplace that had the same lack of scent as the bed. There was a hint of it by the door, which had been mostly overpowered by his, Em's, and Darlene's scents. But the kitchen and living room both only smelled of Em. He got a hint in the bathroom but nothing more. It seemed the activity was mostly confined to the bedroom.

He studied the rips in the fabric. It didn't look like any knife had done it, everything was too jagged. He knew what his claws could do, and he would guess it would look something like this if he chose to destroy bedding.

Despite what he had seen in movies and on TV, Andre didn't have the ability to summon his claws when he was in his human form. He and his pack seemed to be gaining new abilities, but he hadn't yet gained that talent. He hoped one day he did. It would be really useful now. Because his only choice if he wanted to see if the claw marks matched what a wolf could do was to shift completely and try and make some of his own.

He considered it. But shifting and then shifting back would exhaust him, and it would show him something he was pretty sure he already knew. He knew what claw marks looked like. And it wasn't like he was trying to prove that they were exactly the same as him.

Something with claws was after Em, and it could get to her anywhere.

That was the point of attacking her room. No security could stop it.

At least that had been the case before he showed up. Now this clawed beast had a new foe, and it was going to wish it had never threatened Em after Andre was done with it.

8

Em watched Andre work closer than she should have. He had the kind of stalking grace she would expect to see if he was in his animal form. But she had never seen him in his wolf skin. And she realized she wanted to.

She'd spent a lot of time researching wolves in the month since she'd discovered that werewolves were real. For a day she had fallen down the rabbit hole of believing outdated research on alphas and betas and omegas. In that structure, she thought Andre would be an alpha even if he was currently following the orders of Jericho Gibson. If that research had been correct, he wouldn't have stuck around for long.

But things were far more complex than a leadership structure broken down and based on rule by the strongest. She didn't doubt Andre could take just about anyone in a fight. But maybe he still had some things to learn about leading people.

She shook her head. Wild wolves organized themselves in family structures not unlike humans, with a mom and a dad and the baby wolves. Easy to understand, if a little disappointing for not explaining some of the vagaries of human existence.

Em really had to stop thinking about wild wolves. Andre was a human who could turn into a wolf. That was it.

"Do you have any ideas?" she asked, if only so it wouldn't seem so weird that she couldn't stop looking at him.

He was standing by her bed, and she tried really hard not to imagine what it would look like if he was laying down naked in it.

Damn it. And there was that image in her head. His skin would look good in her sheets. Pressed up against her. Pressing into her. Hot hands stroking her flesh as his coc—

No. She wasn't going to do that. She couldn't remember the last time she had wanted a man this much, but she didn't get to have him. She didn't even *like* him.

If she was in a more self-destructive period of her life, she might have suggested they fuck just to get it out of their systems. But that never worked, and

Andre was here for a reason. She was going to take the help he had to give her and nothing else.

"There's nothing," said Andre, frustration lacing his words. He glared at the sheets as if he could intimidate them into confessing.

"No evidence?" Most of her ideas with evidence gathering came from Law and Order, CSI, and other popular police dramas. Not exactly something that would stand up in court. Or something that would give them a clue on how to investigate a supernatural phenomenon. But there were TV shows for that, too.

"No. There's *nothing*." He emphasized the word as if instead of nothing, he truly meant something.

"What do you mean?" Thinking about werewolves and magic was hurting her brain.

Andre struggled for a moment before he seemed to figure out what he wanted to say. "Everything has a scent. And ever since... you know... my sense of smell has improved. Sometimes that is *not* a gift." He shuddered at a memory he didn't share.

She had to smile at that. She didn't know how long he'd stuck around in the military before being discharged, but if his senses had been heightened while living in the barracks, that had to have been a nightmare. She had a feeling that army guys could smell really bad.

He continued. "But your bed and the costume

don't have any scent whatsoever. It's like a void. I've never encountered something like that."

Now she was beginning to understand. He wasn't just talking about something being super clean. "That doesn't sound like a werewolf. I assume one would have a scent." She wondered how different it was than what she could smell. Was it just more? Or was there something indescribable about it?

"A regular werewolf, if there is such a thing, would have a scent," he confirmed. He crouched beside the bed and took another sniff before standing back up. Then he looked over at her and… was that a *blush?* Maybe he felt a bit self conscious for doing something inhuman in front of her.

But she needed him because he wasn't completely human. And she needed to think outside the box. "Ghost werewolf?" It sounded ridiculous even to her own ears as she suggested it, but what else was she supposed to think? They were already in a position where werewolves were the norm.

Andre pursed his lips and considered. Finally, he shrugged. "Maybe. I don't know if ghosts exist. But it's something with claws and something that doesn't have a scent. I'll try and do research. But in the meantime, I think you should cancel tonight's concert."

What did he say? "What?" There was no way she heard that right. "There are thousands of people that are already on their way. They would murder me way more than some sort of ghost werewolf if I canceled tonight."

But his jaw was set and all that sexy—no, not sexy — intensity was pointed her way. "This thing could attack you. Just say you have... exhaustion... or whatever it is you pop stars say that you have when you don't want to perform."

Asshole! And things had been going so well. "First off, I'm a rock star, not a pop star. It doesn't matter, but let's be specific. Second of all, I am physically fine and I don't want rumors swirling that I'm about to go into rehab, or get plastic surgery, or that I'm pregnant, or any of the other dozens of rumors that will swirl if I cancel a concert at the last minute because of *exhaustion*. I'm not exhausted. I'm fine." And some stupid ghost werewolf was not going to keep her from performing. It could scare her, but it would not intimidate her.

Andre let out a sound of frustration that verged on a wolfish growl. "I don't care why you cancel. Say it's technical difficulties. Set the damn concert venue on fire if you have to. But you should *not* go on stage tonight."

"I went on stage last night and it was fine." She'd been a bit freaked, but that had all melted away as one song bled into another.

"You went on stage last night, and today it

attacked your bedroom. That's an escalation. Clearly you can see that." His eyes were a bit wild as he made his points.

As their words got heated, they got closer and closer to one another. It was like they kept being pulled into each other's orbit.

Why couldn't she resist getting close to this man? He was infuriating. She had no doubt he would do something extreme to cancel the concert if he could.

And there was no way she was going to let him.

"So you're saying you can't protect me?" she challenged. He was the one who insisted on staying. So he could do his damn job. "Canceling is a big deal. I can't do it. Find a way to keep me safe."

Andre reared back and began to pace. "Did anything happen like this before you got to this town? You've been here for nearly a week, right?"

And she was supposed to have enjoyed staying in one place. Ghost werewolves had a way of messing things up. "That's right. We roll out tomorrow. And nothing weird happened beforehand. I mean, nothing other than the normal tour weirdness that happens occasionally."

"Normal tour weirdness?" he asked, one eyebrow raised.

It was such a part of tour life that it took Em a minute to figure out what had to be explained. "Stuff goes wonky. It's not magical. This was the first time that anything had been clawed up like this."

That answer didn't satisfy him. "Then why did you call Stasia right away? Seems a little strange to call for help after one incident."

"Did you see the size of those claws? And I've been having bad dreams." She hated to admit it. But he had asked so she would answer. "I usually just collapse in exhaustion after shows. But for the last week or so, I've felt like something's been chasing me. Could just be regular bad dreams. Happens all the time."

He made a sound of acknowledgment, neither agreeing nor disagreeing. And then he got quiet, eyes scraping over the room as he thought. "I'm going to need to talk to Darlene. I don't know how to keep you safe from a werewolf ghost, but I'll do my best."

"If we're lucky, it's just localized to the city and it'll go away once I move on." She hoped. Maybe the hotel was haunted by a ghost werewolf and that was the problem.

What had her life come to?

"We," he corrected.

"We who?" She had a sinking feeling she knew what he meant.

"You're stuck with me until this thing is resolved." And the way Andre said it, it sounded like a threat.

9

ANDRE NEEDED to let Em walk out of this room. Right now. They were standing close. Any closer and it would be an embrace.

That was what his wolf wanted. No. Demanded. He wanted to kiss her. He wanted to leave his mark on her so that anyone who saw her knew that she was his.

He wanted to claim her.

He was going insane. Em breathed heavily, and he could see the argument swirling in her eyes. Did she really think he wouldn't stay with her until this thing was resolved? Did she really think he could be gotten rid of so easily?

He couldn't walk away.

And now he felt a bit of sympathy for Owen. He hadn't understood what his friend went through when he took the job protecting Stasia. If it was anything like this it was no wonder…

No. Andre wouldn't think like that. This wasn't the same. Em wasn't his mate. This wasn't werewolf magic.

But the word mate echoed through his brain, and his inner wolf rumbled with satisfaction.

Mate.

His.

Not going to happen.

"You don't need to come with me," Em insisted. A line formed between her brows, and he wanted to reach out and smooth it out just to see how she'd react.

Andre took a deep breath, pulling her scent deep into his lungs. With the way the scent had been stripped out of her room by whatever beast had marked up her bed, her scent was even stronger than normal and he reveled in it. "You're not getting rid of me," he repeated.

"So you would fight Darlene if I kicked you out?" She crossed her arms and her face was full of the challenge.

He wondered if she would really do it. And he wondered how he would respond. He wasn't about to fight a human. He was stronger, faster, and better trained. He wasn't going to hurt someone. And he didn't think Em would make him.

Still, she was fighting him. "I will report if anything else goes weird. You don't need to interrupt your life for me." She leaned back as if she were going to step away from him, and Andre wrapped his fingers around her arm to keep her close. He wasn't holding her tightly. If she struggled at all, she could get away. But she didn't struggle. And she stopped trying to back up.

"We both know that's not good enough." He didn't want to imagine what would happen if things escalated from vandalism to violence.

"It has to be." She didn't want to back down.

But his will was just as strong as hers. "You need a keeper." The words were a mistake. He knew that. And yet it was true. Couldn't she see that no one could protect her as well as he could?

"We both know you don't want to keep me." She raised one eyebrow in challenge.

His fingers tightened on her arm, just a little, just a reminder. But Andre didn't know what to say to that. Yesterday, he would have agreed. Two hours ago, he would have agreed. But now? Now keeping her safe was the first thing on his mind. Or possibly the second if the bed was in his line of sight. And he wasn't thinking of ghost werewolves when he saw it. "I think you would be surprised by what I want," he finally said.

She snorted, and that broke some of the spell that

held them close. "You want what all guys want. Being a werewolf doesn't make you that special."

Should he be offended by that? His face scrunched up in concentration, but he decided it was a good enough joke to take in stride. And he had seen the desire in her eyes. No matter what they felt for each other some of the time, they both were feeling a carnal desire. One he had little doubt would flare up into a conflagration if they were alone together for long enough.

And he wanted to burn.

"What does Gibson say about you staying around for so long?" She changed tack, still trying to be rid of him.

Andre shrugged; he'd made his choice and he wasn't walking away. "He knows I'm here. He can call me if he needs me." They weren't exactly swimming in jobs. Their bodyguarding outfit was new and worked on a referral basis. That meant sometimes they went weeks without an assignment. Between Gibson's family money and the payments the military had given them to buy their silence, they could manage with all the down time.

Em's shoulders slumped as she gave in. "Fine. But if you cause trouble or make things more difficult than they should be, you're gone." She held up a hand before he could argue. "You're not the only werewolf in the world. I can always call one of your friends. You just said you don't have a job going right now. So piss me off and I'll get… Rowe… to come watch over me."

It took her a moment to remember that name, but his wolf bristled at the suggestion and he had to bite back a growl. He wasn't going to let Leland Rowe get his dirty paws on his… on Em.

Not happening.

"You're stuck with me, sweetheart," he declared, and he couldn't stop the grin that spread across his face at the thought. She might be indignant, but she was still his… to protect. That was all.

She rolled her eyes. "Sweetheart. Are we really doing that, honeybun?"

It was game on.

Andre's place in her life—for now—was apparently decided. "If I don't get back to the venue soon, Melinda is going to murder me. And then the concert definitely will be canceled. So let's go." She led him out of the room. And Andre realized his mistake right as she was opening the door.

He reached out and pulled her back. "I go through doors first. You know how this works."

She heaved a sigh and rolled her eyes. "This is a secure floor. I don't have bodyguards around me twenty-four/seven."

Maybe she should. But Andre was learning, and he kept that thought to himself.

He stepped out into the hall and she followed right after him. And before Andre could take two steps, a bright flash of white light distracted him.

He thought it was the werewolf ghost—and they really had to come up with a better term than that—but then he heard footsteps pounding down the hall and saw a form retreat through an emergency exit.

"Fucking paparazzi." Em scowled and yelled something so creatively insulting after the man that Andre was impressed.

He was ready to take off after the guy, but her hand on his arm stopped him.

"Let him go," she said, sounding defeated. "It's more of a story if we fight it. Come on. We have to go."

ANDRE'S MUSCLES bunched under Em's fingertips, and she was sure he was going to ignore her command and chase off after the paparazzo anyway. She held on a little tighter, just to keep him from getting any ideas.

"I could still catch him," he said. "I'm definitely faster than his ass." His eyes had taken on that golden werewolf sheen, and there was a sharpness to his features that she hadn't seen before. If the vulture had stuck around for just a bit longer, he would've gotten a hell of a shot. Or he might have been eaten by a hungry werewolf.

That wasn't an on-the-job risk he could anticipate.

Em almost smiled, but the violation of her privacy was too new. "It doesn't matter. Those assholes back up their data immediately. The picture is already in the cloud. It's no big deal. I promise." It wasn't a huge deal. She wasn't lying. But there would be rumors of a new man in her life swirling before the day was over.

Potentially annoying. And Andre would hate the speculation that was bound to come his way. But there was nothing to be done about it now.

A growl rumbled in the back of Andre's throat, and his features were even sharper. As were his teeth. His hold on his human form seemed to be slipping as anger at the paparazzo suffused him.

That couldn't happen. She needed him to be a man right now, not a wolf.

Em backed him up into an alcove a little bit down the hall. He let her lead him, she was under no illusions about that. But she needed him out of sight until he got control over his features.

She slid her hands up so they were gripping his biceps; she would have been pinning him in place if she were stronger. His hands landed on her hips and they were close enough to kiss. She froze as the realization hit her.

This was really an embrace. Anything before she could have lied to herself. But now they were just a breath away from a kiss. And Em wanted to lean in and steal it. She wanted to know what Andre tasted like.

She wanted it all.

And the smart part of herself wanted to back away. This was madness. What kind of person was she that she was even more attracted to Andre when he was barely holding onto his humanity? When he was showing the monster that lived within him?

But he wasn't a monster. His wolf was rising to the surface to protect her. Just as the man was dedicated to doing.

And it was clearer than ever that he was right.

This floor was supposed to be secure, and yet a photographer had captured a money shot. Andre had been able to sneak backstage like it was nothing. She had gaping holes in her security and more to worry about than just a ghost werewolf.

One of her hands slid up his arm and cupped right along his jaw, cradling his face in her fingers. Andre's eyes drifted shut and he leaned into the touch. His stubble scraped against her palm, and it was more erotic than the most intimate caress. She could imagine what it would feel like between her thighs.

She pulled her hand away.

She had to get over this. This was adrenaline induced. First the attack last night, then the discovery of the attack today, then the paparazzo. It was all crashing over her and making her feel things that she wasn't supposed to be feeling. That she couldn't afford to feel.

"I should get to sound check," she told him, but she didn't back away, and her other hand was still on his bicep.

His hands were still on her hips. "You said Melinda would kill you if you were late," he agreed, but made no move to pull away.

Their gazes locked. Her eyes flicked down to his lips, and his tongue darted out to wet his, making them even more pink and inviting.

One kiss. What could it hurt?

Her career. Her sanity. Her life.

Her heart?

That was an organ that Em hadn't been thinking with for the past hour or so. No matter how much she wanted Andre on a physical level, she doubted there would be more.

This was crazy werewolf lust. Clearly it happened to some women and she just had to find a way to deal with it.

But it was more than lust for Stasia. They used the word that Em was scared to even *think*. There was no way she and Andre shared the same connection, no matter how scorching and fast things burned between them.

Some people were just hot for one another. And she could accept that was the situation here. But she refused to let it go farther.

She had to be the sane one.

"I have to get to sound check," she said more firmly. But her hand only squeezed harder against him.

Andre pulled on her hips just a bit and shifted her an inch forward. Her chest brushed against his, and her nipples tightened with want. If she arched any closer, she would feel his cock and it would be hard. She was sure of it.

This was bad. And deliciously good. She wanted him bad enough that she almost pulled him back towards her suite, sound check be damned. His eyes had shifted back to their normal color and his features had lost some of that sharpness. He was human again.

But his eyes were still hungry like the…

No. She refused to think that.

But thinking of the song made laughter bubble up in her throat and broke the sensual spell that held her in place.

"What?" Andre asked in confusion. And his confusion seemed to banish some of his lust.

She shouldn't say it. He would think she was silly or wasn't taking things seriously. Or he might just not like the joke.

But the thought of annoying him was enough to make the words come out. "You looked hungry. Like the wolf."

Andre groaned. "I can't believe you." He gave her

a playful shove, nothing that could actually hurt her, and she stepped back.

She sang a few lines, and she was pretty sure that if there was any danger near her, it came from the werewolf who looked ready to cover her mouth with his giant paw to shut her up.

She sang the lines and swaggered down the hall toward the elevator, nearly jumping in shock when Andre joined her for the rest of the chorus.

Who knew the werewolf was capable of humor? Or that he could sing?

Her heart beat a little faster and threatened to open up and invite him in.

She was in trouble. If Andre smiled and sang and acted like a person, she might just start having feelings. And she couldn't afford to do that.

Maybe she needed to give Stasia a call. This had all started with crazy werewolf pheromones, and there had to be some way to resist them.

She hoped. Because giving into the temptation that was Andre Gordon could be the most dangerous thing she'd ever considered.

11

ANDRE WATCHED from the wings as Em began her sound check. No one except a few crew members were in the audience, but it would have been impossible to tell from the intensity of her performance. She gave it her all. And it was amazing to watch.

Andre hadn't been to a concert in years. After being turned he had been concerned that his heightened senses would be set off by the sensory overload that came from a performance.

But his entire being was focused on Em. All of his senses attuned. And he was doing fine.

Or perhaps not fine.

Being captivated by her meant he was shirking his duty. He was supposed to keep her safe. He was supposed be watching for suspicious activity or ghost werewolves, not listening to her belt out a chorus about getting revenge after being cheated on.

Who the fuck would cheat on her?

Whoever she was singing about, he was glad they were gone. Not that he should be thinking like that. She wasn't his, no matter how much he lusted after her.

He forced himself to turn away. He walked deeper backstage to try and get a feel for her security. And as suspected, it was a nightmare.

They weren't focused the way they needed to be. But Andre looked at this through a soldier's eyes. A civilian security force had different goals. But he had a feeling he would need to talk to Darlene. He couldn't tell her exactly why he was around. She wouldn't believe him if he uttered the words ghost werewolf, but she should've never let that paparazzo upstairs.

Had someone been paid off? Was it negligence? He wanted to get to the bottom of it, but it wasn't his job. He would tell Darlene about what had happened. She needed to know. But he had to leave it at that.

For now.

And that was a duty he could do later. First he had to report back. This wasn't an official job, but the others needed to know what was going on, especially the supernatural angle.

Ever since Stasia had been changed, they were paying more attention to the ways they were changing and the realities of being werewolves in this world. Gibson had put out feelers to some of his old contacts and they were trying to gather as much information as possible, even if it was coming in at a snail's pace.

This development was the biggest thing that had happened since they were turned, and Andre had no way of knowing if werewolves had anything to do with it.

He went back to Em's dressing room since it was quiet enough to make the call and tried to get in touch with Gibson. But the major didn't answer, and this wasn't something that Andre was going to leave in a message. He could call back later, but he had to talk to someone. And Stasia would be desperate to know if things were okay with Em. So he gave Owen a call.

He absently traced over the gouges in the table that matched the torn outfit and the bedsheets. They weren't that deep. They could have been made with a knife or maybe even a pen, given enough time. But Andre doubted it.

His friend answered on the first ring. "I expected to hear from you sooner," said Owen, but there wasn't any accusation in his words. He was a chipper guy, almost always upbeat and expecting it from everyone else.

Andre had no idea how the two of them had become best friends. "It's been an interesting couple of hours." He told Owen about the torn up costume and the bedding and about the strange lack of scent.

For half a moment he considered mentioning the explosive attraction between himself and Em, but he held that back. *That* had nothing to do with the ghost werewolf. And it wasn't like Em was his mate.

His wolf grumbled at that denial; it had other ideas.

It was none of Owen's damned business. So Andre kept quiet on that front.

"A ghost werewolf?" Owen was skeptical, and if Andre wasn't mistaken there was a hint of laughter in his tone.

"I know it sounds fucked up. What else would you call it? It looks like it has claws and it doesn't smell like anything. No one's seen anything." But Andre would need to see if there was security footage.

"Are you sure it's not just Febreeze?" Owen asked gently.

"I know what Febreeze smells like. Everyone knows what Febreeze smells like. Why do you keep asking that?" He'd had this nose on his head for thirty-three years. He knew what things smelled like.

"Keep asking? I only asked that once." There was a smile in Owen's voice. Maybe that was why they were friends. He didn't get mad when Andre lashed out.

"Em asked the same thing. It's not Febreeze. It's not anything. It is a void of scent. I don't know if the ghost did it or if there is some sort of magic spell that could erase a scent. I'm working in the dark here." He didn't know what kind of magic existed. Clearly there was some type that could turn people into wolves. But beyond that, it was a mystery.

Owen let out a whistle. "You think we turn into ghosts when we die?" he mused.

Now was not the time for jokes. "Are you suggesting that she's being *haunted* by a werewolf?"

"You're the one that said werewolf ghost." Of course Owen had to point it out.

Indeed he had, but Andre was pretty sure this wasn't an *actual* ghost, if such a thing even existed. "Run it by the others," he requested. "Maybe we'll get some ideas out of them."

Owen let the jokes drop. "Will do. Do you need backup? Rowe is eager to head out and help you."

Andre didn't growl, and he was proud of that. But he was quiet for longer than he should have been. And Owen definitely noticed.

"I'm fine," Andre finally said.

"Anything else you want to tell me?" Owen

prodded, and Andre could hear the annoying grin on his face. The bastard.

"Nope," and the P popped as he said it. Emphasis enough that that line of questioning was closed.

"You sure?" Owen just had to poke and poke and poke.

There were a lot of things Andre could say, each more incriminating than the last. So instead he pulled his phone away from his ear and clicked the button to hang up harder than he needed to. Thankfully he wasn't strong enough to crack his own screen. That would be annoying.

And even though the connection between them was broken, he was almost positive he could hear Owen's laugh. Yeah, Owen suspected something was going on. And eventually he would start questioning things.

But Andre wasn't going to let anything happen. Not between himself and Em, and especially not letting any danger get to her. It meant he had to stay close by her. But he was a professional. It wouldn't be a problem.

His phone dinged with an incoming text message. "Will check in on evil werewolf ghost. Remember to use protection."

And then another text. "Condoms. I mean condoms. Don't know what protection you need from an evil werewolf ghost."

"Fuck you, dude." Andre silenced his phone and shoved it in his pocket before he could send any sort of reply.

Yeah, he wasn't hiding his feelings at all. And he couldn't imagine what Stasia's opinion on all of this would
be.

But Em could handle her sister. And with that thought in mind, he headed back to the wings of the stage to watch the end of her sound check.

This was the kind of temptation he would let himself give in to. Hopefully it would allow him to stave off his worst desires.

Sound check went just as it was supposed to, and for the first time all day, Em was really ready for the show that night. She let thoughts of ghost werewolves and sexy living werewolves slip out of her head as she fell down into her own music.

She thanked her band as she did after every performance, and her guitarist Jerry had a few questions before she was finally able to leave. She felt drawn like a magnet to Andre, but it was Vi, the same crew member she'd seen earlier that day, who caught her attention.

The purple-haired woman was fiddling with one of the speakers, a look of intense concentration and frustration on her face.

"By Hecate's ghost, I will defeat you," Vi muttered

at the machine as she smacked one side and then shook her hand as if she'd been shocked.

What was that exclamation? "Is everything okay?" Em asked. Melinda was sure to know everything that was going wrong, but Em liked to keep track of what she could. It was better to know than to be surprised later.

Vi slapped the side of the speaker again and threw her tool down on the ground. "It was a bit buzzy. If I can't fix it, I'll have one of the technicians come and take a look. Should be all good for the show."

That was normal enough. She almost asked Vi what she had said earlier, but realized it was none of her business. People said weird things all the time and it wasn't like it was anything offensive.

Em had a schedule to keep to. The concert was creeping closer, and soon fans would be lining up around the building. Her opening act no doubt needed to get situated, and it was her job to stay out of the way at this point.

It would probably be a good use of her time to track down Darlene and make sure that Andre was on whatever list he needed to be on. With that in mind, she turned away from Vi, but paused as she saw something strange moving in the shadows of the stage.

At first she thought it was Jerry or one of her other bandmates. But Kristin and Floyd were all still on the stage and whoever—or whatever—was moving was too small to be Jerry. It could have been a crew member. But she had never seen a crew member move like that.

And for a second, Em forgot about all of the dangers that were haunting her and stepped towards the shadow just like some stupid girl in a horror movie.

Vi's hand on her shoulder held her back. "What is it?" the crew member demanded. She sounded completely different than she had just a moment ago, all serious, as if it wasn't just a weird shadow.

Em's heart started beating hard, and she wished that Andre was at her side. Where was he? Was that the thing that had destroyed her stuff? Or was she freaking out over nothing?

The shadow moved, and suddenly Em was sure it was more than just a shadow. She made out four legs and a bunched-up body as it ran toward her. She was frozen in place, unable to move out of the way and sure she was about to meet her death.

And then Andre was there, charging past her and straight for the beast as if running into danger meant nothing.

Em wanted to chase after him. That shadow beast

was scary, something out of a nightmare. She was sure it had teeth as big as her arm and probably untold powers. She knew it was nothing natural.

The danger was real and Andre was headed straight for it.

"What was that?" Vi asked. She was standing a step in front of Em, which was strange, because she'd been behind her a moment before Em saw the beast.

Had Vi moved to get a closer look? Or had she purposely put herself in front of Em?

And what was she doing here? It wasn't her job to repair the speakers.

Vi met her eyes, and the bright blue of the crew member's eyes seemed to shift to something deeper, something almost purple for a moment.

"What was that thing?" Vi repeated insistently.

Em blinked hard and shook her head. Clearly she was more out of it than she thought if she was questioning every single person on the crew. She didn't know what Vi's responsibilities were. She probably wasn't doing anything weird. And Em definitely did *not* want to explain werewolves to her. "Probably just a cat or something. Maybe a stray dog. I'm sure it's fine."

She strained to hear any hint of Andre's presence, but wherever he had run, it was far away.

He had to be okay. He had come to protect her, and she didn't know how she would manage if it was her fault that he got hurt.

13

ANDRE RACED after the beast like the fate of the world depended on it. He dodged around equipment and vaulted over a bench as the monster turned down a hallway and moved further into the darkness.

Andre didn't know if he was being led somewhere or if the beast was moving on instinct. It only occurred to him once he was far away from Em and the rest of the humans that there could be a pack of these things waiting for him somewhere.

It didn't matter. As long as it wasn't near Em. Maybe he was cocky, but Andre was willing to put his skills to the test against a gang of these things any day.

In the darkness, it was difficult to make out the beast. It looked sort of like a wolf that was covered in black fur that seemed to bleed into the darkness.

But the dim light of the hallway wasn't completely black, and Andre could see it moving in the shadows.

How had no one noticed it? It was a full-sized wolf. Even a stray dog should've caught attention. But it had gotten all the way to the stage with no one saying a word.

Magic? Or more lax security?

The wolf's growl reverberated down the hall, and Andre saw that he had it cornered. There was a set of closed doors that the wolf charged at, but it froze before actually running into the heavy steel. The doors remained stubbornly closed. He didn't know where they led, but at least the wolf couldn't go any further.

Andre wanted to shift into his other form. If he did that, then he might have a better chance of injuring the wolf. As a man, he didn't have sharp teeth or claws to fight the beast. But it would take time to shift, time that he didn't have. And it wasn't like he had never fought a wolf in his human form.

It was a game he and the rest of his pack mates liked to play from time to time. And it was a game that Andre was pretty good at.

"Easy there, puppy," he said in the same sort of conciliatory tone he might have used with a frightened dog. If he could stop the fight before it started, that would be even better. He didn't know why this animal was attacking Em. He couldn't be certain that it *was* this animal.

But as he got close, he realized it must be. He'd been too preoccupied during the chase to notice it, but though the beast looked like a wolf and moved like a wolf, it didn't smell like a wolf.

It didn't smell like anything.

No living being that Andre had ever encountered was like that.

Everything had a scent. Except for this beast.

The wolf reared around, and yellow eyes flashed in the dim light. And that was strange too. They were like gemstones embedded in his face, flat and yet almost sparkling. They didn't look like normal eyes. There was something off about this beast.

And Andre was beginning to wonder if it was even a wolf at all.

But it had teeth like a wolf and it bared them at him. The growl might have scared another man. but Andre just fell back into a defensive stance and grinned. With the way tension had tightened his body all day, he'd been yearning for a fight. And this wolf was just the beast to give it to him.

He had to stop it before anyone came this way. And not just for safety. After that cameraman got a shot of him and Em, there were sure to be rumors swirling, and this was another way he could protect her. Who knew what kind of rumors would swirl if they saw a wolf backstage at her concert? He could at the very least stop *that* from happening.

The wolf charged, and Andre let go of the thoughts of protecting Em's reputation. There was nothing but the fight.

And the wolf knew how to do it. It snapped with those vicious teeth and swiped at him with its claws. Andre fought back, doing his best to avoid all of the sharp bits and aiming for the wolf's tender belly and its throat.

He didn't have his firearm with him. That might have made this whole thing easier.

But he had a knife. And he had pulled it without thought and used it as if it were his own claws. But no matter how deftly he wielded it and how sure he was that he had hit the wolf, no blood dripped from its fur.

Andre wished he could say the same. A rough swipe of claws caught him on the shoulder, and the wolf's teeth had scraped through his jeans and into the flesh of his thigh.

He would be hurting soon. And the wolf showed no sign of flagging.

The wolf growled again and snapped his teeth, and this time, Andre let out a threatening growl of his own.

The wolf froze. Their gazes locked, and Andre tried to see any sort of intelligence, any consciousness, in the wolf. It didn't fight like a wild animal.

He was beginning to think it was nothing of the sort.

Another growl rumbled out of Andre, and the wolf shrank back. He advanced on it, knife at his side and ready to try to inflict as much damage as he could.

The wolf started forward and Andre dodged to the side to avoid its charge, but he misjudged the distance and slammed into the wall.

The lights flashed on overhead, and he realized he must have hit the light switch. He flinched from the sudden brightness and spun around, ready to face the wolf again.

But all he saw was a wisp of black smoke that quickly dissolved.

No wolf.

And the door behind where it had been remained closed.

Andre tested it and found it locked. The wolf hadn't gone that way.

And he was beginning to think it might have dissolved in a puff of smoke.

But it had been real enough. The blood dripping down his leg and soaking his shirt was proof.

A wolf that could turn into shadow. He needed to find Em. He didn't know what she could do, but she needed to know. This was more information, and they needed to strategize.

One thing was certain, he wasn't letting her sit in the dark.

14

EM EVENTUALLY HAD ENOUGH of waiting and went to go look for Andre. She wasn't eager to find the shadow wolf or whatever it was, but as long as Andre was there, she knew she'd be safe. And she didn't know what she would do if something had happened to him because of her.

He was her bodyguard. Whether she liked it or not. But that didn't mean that she wished any harm coming to him.

Just the opposite.

She didn't have to go far before she found him staggering down the hallway, one hand covered in blood where he clutched his shoulder.

She rushed to him. "Oh my God, are you okay?" It was stupid. He was bleeding. Of course he wasn't okay.

Andre gave a tight grimace. Without a second thought, Em got close and scooped herself under his uninjured arm, leading him back to her dressing room. If that photographer had been around now, he would've gotten a hell of a photo. But someone had to be smiling down on Em, since the hallway was strangely deserted.

She got them into her dressing room and set him gently down on her couch. The fabric was dark, but she wasn't particularly concerned about leaving stains at the moment. There was a small first-aid kit under her dressing table and she grabbed it, flipping it open and looking for supplies.

"You don't need to do that," Andre called over her shoulder. He was still sitting down, and there was a roughened edge to his voice that came from the pain of whatever had happened. "It will heal soon. I heal fast."

Still, Em turned around with a bottle of saline and some gauze bandages. "So you know how fast you heal when a ghost werewolf attacks you?" she challenged with more vigor than she was feeling. Her hands were shaking, and the tremor threatened to move through her whole body. This was *real*. It wasn't just some torn clothing or bedding. It was torn skin. Torn Andre. And Em was on the edge of freaking out.

Andre gave her a pained grin. "Okay, this is new.

But it *is* healing." And then he pulled off his shirt to show her.

Em's mouth went dry. She had seen plenty of shirtless men before. It was almost a requirement of her job. But Andre was a force unto himself. Even with a trickle of blood reminding her of what he had just gone through, she still wanted to feel the hard planes of his chest against her hands.

And her tongue.

But she wasn't going to do that. Because he needed help.

"Wolf got your tongue?" Andre asked.

Oh, she wanted to slap him. It was completely juvenile. Why did she feel a bit like a little girl being teased on the playground? But then Andre shifted in his seat and winced. And thoughts of slapping and teasing fled.

She knelt on the couch beside him and soaked one of the bandages in saline, using it to wipe away some of the blood from the wound. It was nasty, but he was right. At this point it didn't look like something a wild animal had done to him. It appeared like the kind of scratch he could get by accidentally catching on a nail or some other type of easy to explain injury.

He placed his hand over hers and stopped her from moving. "I'm okay, I promise." Their eyes locked again, and she could feel the weight of it. If he wasn't okay, he was a great liar. But she didn't think he would lie about this. He was here to keep her safe.

"Did you kill it?" she asked. What had her life come to where that was a question she had to ask?

His expression was grim as he shook his head. "It disappeared."

She didn't know what he meant by that, but she was more concerned about his healing wounds. "Not before giving you these nasty gouges."

"Unfortunately not."

"How did it disappear? Where? Did it run outside?" She hoped there wasn't some ghost werewolf tormenting her fans, but someone probably would have said something by this point.

"I mean it *disappeared*," he repeated, stressing the word. "One minute we were fighting and the next it was like smoke. Just gone."

"Like magic." It wasn't a question. She could accept werewolves. Even werewolves created by magic. But magic itself was still difficult to wrap her mind around.

"Yes." He shifted again, and his eyes scrunched down as he thought. "I slammed into the wall and hit the light switch," he said. "That's when it disappeared. It was pretty dark before then."

"So you think it's afraid of light? Or maybe there is some sort of... magic stuff... that means it can't attack in the light?" This was not the kind of logic she was used to using, but they needed an advantage over the thing.

Andre wasn't so quick to agree. "I wouldn't set our expectations there. We don't want to draw that conclusion and have it bite us in the ass. But I *would* encourage you to keep the lights on."

Now was not the time to explain how the lights for the concert would work. Maybe Em was being grossly naïve, but if there was something controlling this ghost werewolf, she had to assume it wouldn't attack her during the concert.

Magic-using people probably didn't want magic to be widely known if they hadn't revealed themselves by now. And having a ghost werewolf attack her in the middle of a concert would be one way to announce magic to the world.

"Yes, I still think you should cancel the concert," Andre answered the unasked question.

For some reason that made Em huff out a little laugh. "And I'm still not going to do it. I really don't think it will attack me in front of so many people."

"It just attacked you in front of the entire crew," he pointed out.

"No it didn't," she responded. "It was sniffing around the equipment. You chased it. We don't know if it was going to attack me."

"You're playing with your life." His stare was almost intense enough to make her back down.

Almost. "Then protect me. You're doing a good job so far."

Andre groaned, and she tried really hard not to imagine what kind of guttural sounds he would make if they were in bed together.

There was a knock on her door, but before Em could say anything, Darlene was opening it.

"There's no sign of that photographer anymore," she said. Then her eyes traveled over to Andre, who was pulling his shirt back on. Darlene looked between the two of them for several moments, but didn't ask what Em had been doing with a shirtless man in her dressing room.

Darlene could draw her own conclusions.

"Andre is going to be staying on with us for a bit," Em informed her, ignoring the implications of their positions. She was an adult woman. She could have as many shirtless men in her dressing room as she wanted. "Can you get him a hotel room for tonight?"

Darlene grimaced and shook her head. "No can do. Hotel's fully booked. He'll have to bunk up with one of the other security members."

Em didn't need to see Andre's face to know that was a no go. "My suite is big enough for both of us. He can sleep on the couch or we can get a rollaway bed. We'll figure something out." She didn't want to admit that the thought of Andre nearby made her feel better. He could protect her from monsters if he was within yelling distance.

Darlene seemed to be suppressing a grin, as if she assumed that Em was just keeping up appearances. But Em was no blushing maiden and she didn't care if people thought she and Andre were fucking. "Did you need me for something else?"

"It's about time for the concert. You need to start getting ready."

"Can you show Andre the ropes while I'm busy?" she asked. He seemed to be doing fine on his own, but Em didn't mention that.

Darlene nodded.

Em finally looked back to Andre. There was a rip in his shirt where the ghost werewolf had attacked, but it wasn't too bad, and the skin under it seemed to be mostly healed, maybe a little bit red. He gave her a tight smile and a nod. They couldn't speak the truth in front of Darlene, but she knew what Andre would be looking for.

"Have a good show," he told her, even though he wanted her to cancel. "I promise I'll keep you safe."

And the craziest thing of all was that she believed him.

15

DESPITE HIS INITIAL IMPRESSIONS, Andre had to admit that Darlene and her team had a decent security setup. Far from perfect, but in normal circumstances that should have gotten the job done.

And he was here to make sure they could get back to normal circumstances eventually.

Darlene was pissed as hell that the photographer had gotten back to the hotel rooms, but had already identified how it'd happened—he'd paid off a hotel employee—and was working to remedy the situation. She acted quickly, and he had a feeling she might even be useful against the ghost werewolf. She had a good head on her shoulders and seemed highly adaptable.

Not that he was going to say a word about the ghost werewolf. He could still barely think the term without rolling his eyes. But he had seen the beast himself. Shadows and claws and glowing eyes.

It was a threat to Em, somehow. And he wasn't going to let it get any closer.

"She said you were a private investigator?" Darlene asked with a practiced air of indifference.

She was fishing. It wasn't every day that a stranger like him showed up out of the blue and sat shirtless in her boss's dressing room.

Or maybe he was fooling himself. Maybe Em had men in and out of her dressing room—and other areas—all the time.

His wolf bristled under his skin. Oh now, he did not like the sound of that. Em was... he wasn't going down that road. He couldn't ignore the attraction blazing hot between them, but it couldn't come to anything.

And he certainly wasn't going to let himself start having thoughts that would only lead to emotional agony.

"I needed a new job after I got out of the service." He wasn't going to directly lie to Darlene if he could help it. Lies had a way of adding up, but he would play along with the story Em had given her.

"How long have you been in the business?"

"A couple years." It was how long he had been a bodyguard... and a werewolf. But that was close to private investigating, right? It felt like it. But he was probably fooling himself.

Darlene accepted it. "So what do you think is going on? We've had some weird shit that I can't understand go down."

"I'm trying to figure that out." And he had no idea. "What kind of weird shit?" Em had only told him about the torn clothes and bad dreams. As far as she was concerned, things were otherwise normal.

But Darlene was shaking her head. "I'm sure it's just my imagination. Some places just give me the heebie-jeebies. Like someone's watching me in the dark. Ready to attack. But I think that's just from watching one too many horror flicks."

Or there was a beast stalking the shadows. But Andre didn't say that out loud. There was no need to speak of it yet. If he had to tell her, he would. He just hoped he didn't have to.

"Is it okay if I wander around backstage while the concert's going? I want to get a feel for what goes on." And he wanted to see if the monster showed up again. It was bold and likely to get bolder.

"As long as you stay out of the way of other people. And here," she said, handing him a lanyard with a large plastic badge on it. "Keep that on. It'll let everyone know that you're supposed to be back here."

Andre slipped the lanyard on and didn't remind

her that he had navigated backstage for hours just fine without any form of identification.

"There's a spot in the wings where you can watch the show," she told him. "Just make sure you can't see the audience and that you make way when you need to."

He nodded and took off. It was tempting to go watch the show. He had never been backstage at a concert before. But he had a feeling that Em was right and that the beast would not attack her while she was on stage. At least not yet. It seemed to be escalating, but that was a few steps higher in any game of escalation. It would probably try to get to her in some other way first.

Andre wouldn't let it.

He headed towards the dressing rooms on the thought that the beast had gone to Em's the night before, so why wouldn't it try again? He found Vi standing in front of Em's dressing room door, waving her hands in front of it.

Was she holding a flashlight? Something seemed to be glowing, but he couldn't see what it was. He took a step closer, but before he could confront her, three of Em's backup singers rushed down the hall, probably for a costume change. And even though there was no time for her to get away, Vi was no longer standing there.

That was weird. And Andre didn't like weird.

He approached the door and opened it, sticking his head inside to look to see if Vi was hiding there. But no one was in the room. He could smell Em's scent and his own along with a hint of Darlene's from earlier. There were other scents too, ones he didn't quite recognize. Probably from her makeup people or costuming people. But there wasn't the lack of scent that came from the ghost werewolf... the shadow beast. Yeah, that was better. No scent from the shadow beast.

And he didn't think he caught Vi's scent, though he only remembered that there'd been an odd note to her scent. He couldn't recall exactly what she smelled like.

And that was strange in itself. He had no difficulty memorizing people's scents—it was almost the same as memorizing faces. But Vi was fuzzy in his mind. And he couldn't remember meeting anyone else like that.

He would keep it in mind. Maybe Vi needed to be questioned. After all, she had been on this tour for a while, and at the very least had probably seen some of the weird stuff that Darlene had mentioned.

He wandered backstage some more, but finally ended up in the wings just as Em started one of her more famous hits and the crowd went wild.

He flinched away from the loud noise. Maybe a rock concert wasn't the best place for a werewolf. But since he was on the stage, he was behind the huge speakers that projected her sound out to the thousands of people in the audience, and it meant it wasn't quite as loud as it otherwise would have been.

It hurt. But once Em started singing, the pain faded away as he watched her belt her heart out.

He had thought the performance during sound check was all she had to give. But he hadn't realized just how much she was holding back. He had never seen this side of Em before. There were hints of it. And she always had that irresistible quality to her.

She made him want things. More than just a roll in the sheets. She made him want what he had seen only once before, what he had thought could never exist.

Mate.

Was it fate? Hormones? Was it something quantifiable?

He didn't know if he cared. His wolf wanted to charge out on stage and claim Em in front of all these people so that they would know exactly whose mark she wore.

But she wore no mark. And she was not his. And Andre had to back away from the stage as the song came to a close. One assistant shot him a pointed glare, and he realized he was almost visible to the crowd.

He bled back into the shadows and then retreated

further backstage to look around more for the shadow beast.

He was here for a reason and he had to remember that. Em wasn't his. But he was going to keep her safe.

16

Energy thrummed through Em and she practically skipped back to her hotel room. The audience was all keyed up and their hype only made her feel even more energized. It was like that after a good concert. Performing always made her feel good, even when she was working through an illness or heartbreak.

But nights like this were what the job was made for. The audience carried her along on their excitement, and she gave them every bit of her.

There were no threats when she stood on that stage. There were no photographers hanging around the corner and trying to get money shots. It was just her, her fans, and the music.

She wanted to dance. She wanted to run back on that stage and sing for another hour.

A raucous laugh caught in the back of her throat,

and she perched on the edge of mania. It was a good night.

But after a small meet and greet where she took pictures and signed autographs, she headed back to her hotel room. Another rock star might have gone out on the town and drank until sunrise. But no matter how much energy Em had right now, she knew she would regret that in the morning.

But it was almost worth it.

She unlocked the door to her suite, all the while singing a song she had stuck in her head. It was one that her opening act had performed, and every time she heard it, it stuck with her all night.

Maybe she would cover it. Or maybe they could release a duet of it. She should probably make a note of that. She was pretty sure she had had this thought before. And she wasn't sure for how much longer that opening act would be part of her tour. Sometimes they switched out after a few weeks.

"You seem chipper." Andre sat on the couch in her suite and placed his phone on the side table.

Em almost jumped out of her skin. The excitement of the concert had wiped away the threat of the ghost werewolf, and she had almost forgotten that Andre would be waiting in her room.

And damn did he look good. Liquid heat slid through her veins and settled deep in her core. Maybe she wouldn't go out for a night on the town.

But Andre was right here. And he was as hot as they came.

"It was a good concert." She couldn't keep the smile off her face. This was what she lived for. The first time she had belted out a tune in front of a crowd, she had known that it was what she wanted to do forever. It had taken a bit of work to convince the world that this was where she belonged, but now they knew. Now she was at the top. And she wasn't going to be toppled.

But she could definitely be convinced to be under someone right now.

Someone specific.

"It was a good show," he said. He didn't bother to get up from the couch.

Her brain tingled with curiosity and desire for praise. "You watched?" She didn't know why she was so excited. She knew she had killed it. But the idea that Andre liked it... Well. She wanted him to admit it.

Andre looked at her for several seconds, and his gaze was heavy. "I only watched for a bit. Werewolf ears don't exactly mesh with speakers. But what I saw I enjoyed."

"We can get you earplugs. That might make it better." She had her own that helped muffle the sound of the crowd and the stage and the speakers, along with allowing the sound guys to cue her in and keep her on task. But simple earplugs would probably do the trick for Andre. She knew a lot of the stage crew wore them. And she liked the thought of the werewolf being able to listen to her.

"Maybe I'll get some," he agreed. "I'd like to watch you some more."

Her cheeks heated with an excited blush. She was pretty sure she would like him watching her. "Just ask Melinda. She can do anything."

He nodded. And he was still sitting on that couch.

Why wasn't he coming closer to her? Why wasn't he kissing her? He needed to be doing both of those things right now. Her bed was back there, and it was big and it was soft and it was perfect. And she needed him in it with her.

She needed him *in* her.

So she was going to move this thing along. She was covered in sweat, but she didn't think Andre would mind. She peeled off her shirt and threw it aside.

Andre sat up straighter. "What are you doing?" he asked. There was an edge to his words, a feral hint of the wolf that lived inside him.

She liked that wolf. She wanted to see a bit of his animal come out. She wanted him unrestrained.

She stalked toward him, channeling his predator, and straddled his legs, her knees on the couch and her hands on the back of it, trapping him in place.

"Em…" Was it a warning, or was he begging for more?

"Performance always hypes me up," she said, leaning towards his neck and breathing deep. Wolves cared so much about scent. And she could smell him, but not nearly as much as she was sure he could scent her. She didn't get why they were obsessed with it. Not when there were so many other things to care about. She scraped her teeth along his neck, and Andre shivered.

His hands landed on her hips, but he didn't push her away. He didn't pull her closer either.

Em had to change that. She licked a stripe of skin and could taste his pulse under her tongue.

"Em—" It was a groan, a plea.

And now it was her turn to shiver. She liked the sound of that. She kissed up his jaw and found his lips.

He didn't respond for a moment and then he surrendered to it, one of his hands coming up and cradling her head as he held her close to him and their tongues tangled.

Yes. This was what she needed. He kissed like he had been blessed by some god of lust, and she wanted to know all the wicked things he could do with his tongue. He gave her no mercy. It didn't matter that she was the one sitting on top of him, she had no illusions. He was in control.

And he proved it a moment later when he pulled back with a gasp. "Are you drunk?" he asked with an edge.

"Did you taste any alcohol?" Someone always had a bottle of something backstage, but Em hadn't had anything tonight. "Do you think I'd only want you if I was drunk?" She arched against him, feeling the hard press of his cock underneath his jeans.

Andre pushed her back a bit. "You don't normally like me this much," he said.

"What does like have to do with anything?"

He stared at her for several moments and she could read the challenge, but she didn't know how he wanted her to react.

Finally, he placed both hands back on her hips and pushed her off of him until she was sitting next to him on the couch. "Tell me if you plan to go out tonight. You shouldn't go anywhere alone."

And then he headed to the smaller bathroom in the suite and closed the door behind him. Apparently he didn't care if she was alone in the room.

And Em sank back into the cushions. He didn't want her. No matter what she thought she saw. No matter how he kissed her back. She had to get that through   her head.

Rejection sucked.

17

DESIRE WAS A DRUG, and Andre needed to escape the temptation. As the doorknob clicked closed as he entered the bathroom, he sucked in deep breaths and tried to banish the taste of Em from his mouth.

It was impossible. She was already imprinted on his memory and there was no forgetting it. Not that he really wanted to.

He could turn right around and take her. She was willing. Eager, even. And his cock was more than determined to see her satisfied.

But something stopped him. The energy that was making her ride high would see her crash down in no time. And it may not have been alcohol or drugs that put her in this altered state, but he didn't want to wake up in the morning and see regret in her eyes.

That had happened to him before. Not many times. But enough to send him running.

And maybe that wasn't the only thing that sent him running. He was here to protect her, not fuck her. Sex could screw up everything. And he needed his mind sharp while he did his duty.

His mind wasn't sharp now. And only one part of him was hard. He rubbed the palm of his hand against the erection straining under his jeans and had to bite back a groan. Em might be on the other side of that door, and he didn't want her knowing what he was thinking right now.

What he was doing right now.

Cold shower. That was the responsible thing to do.

Andre stripped off his clothes and let them fall in a pile. He was thankful to see a few towels on the rack over the toilet. Hopefully by the time he got out of the shower, Em would have retreated to her room. There was no need for more temptation.

Because if she kissed him again, he didn't think he could hold himself back.

His hand automatically shifted the shower towards hot water, and as the steam of the spray surrounded him in the room, he couldn't force himself to turn it to a dousing cold. If he couldn't have Em's embrace, at least he could have the embrace of hot water.

He stepped into the shower and felt his muscles begin to relax as the hot water beat down on him.

But not everything relaxed. His cock still stood tall and proud and ready to give Em all the pleasure he knew how to give.

He should be thinking of something else. Of someone else. But she had taken control of him with a single touch and it was like no one else existed.

He tried to ignore his cock. Discipline was a necessary part of his life. But as the water trickled down his body and teased him, he knew there was no other way to get rid of this problem.

She didn't need to know. It wasn't like he was going to tell her. And she couldn't hear him over the rush of the water.

He didn't know why it was taking so long to talk himself into it. There was nothing wrong with doing this.

Nothing wrong, except for the fact that if he walked out the door he could have her.

Andre wrapped his hand around his cock and gave himself a stroke, letting the deep groan escape his throat without a thought.

She would be tighter around him, hot and wet and moaning with desire. If he had her in the shower with him, her legs would be wrapped around his waist and her back against the wall as he plunged into her and pulled out and plunged in and pulled out. The heat of her body and the heat of the shower would melt together until there was nothing but the two of them.

But once they were in bed, she would be on top of him, straddling him just as she had done on the couch.

But this time there would be no clothes between them. Just hot skin and desire.

He stroked harder, faster, but his mind didn't struggle to keep up with the erotic images of Em.

When she went on that stage, she was called Mercy. But she would show him none in the sensual onslaught. And he didn't want mercy from her.

He wanted everything else.

He wanted her over him and under him and beside him. He wanted her lips and her cunt and her ass and her mind and her heart.

Andre groaned again, but this time it wasn't just sexual pleasure. These thoughts were dangerous. He had no rights to her. And it wasn't like she liked him.

Once the mystery was solved, he would walk away, and though they might see each other again every now and then, there would be nothing between them but the memories.

Memories they didn't even have now.

How would she sound when she cried out, her body rippling around him?

How would her kisses change after they had been connected on that fundamental level?

How would she look at him if he owned her heart?

Andre came in a burst of pleasure, the evidence of which the shower quickly washed away.

He leaned against the opposite wall, bracing himself with his arm against the tiles as the water pelted his back.

He needed to find a way to stop thinking of Em like this. He couldn't afford to get distracted, not if it meant risking her life.

But stroking his cock had done nothing but stoke his appetite for her.

He wanted more. He wanted all.

And he couldn't have her. Not when he was the only one that stood between her and some unknown force determined to do her harm.

Eventually the shower stopped and Andre toweled himself off. But he waited for several more minutes until he was absolutely certain that Em had retreated to her bedroom before exiting the bathroom.

Neither of them needed more temptation tonight.

But come morning, he didn't know if he would be able to resist a second time.

1 8

THE ANNOYING CHIME of Em's cell phone finally roused her out of bed. She reached over the side table with blind eyes and slapped around until she finally found it, unhooking it from the charger and blearily reading the message that had forced her awake.

It was from Stasia. "Oh my God, I'm so sorry." And there was a link right after it.

For a second, Em wondered if her sister had been hacked. But curiosity was too great and she clicked on the link, and once the page loaded, she groaned and turned to her side, burying her face in a pillow.

New flame for Mercy?

The rocker was spotted coming out of her swanky hotel room with a new man, name unknown. Sources close to the star confirm he's not a member of her crew. And given the way they've been cozying up, we think sparks might be flying.

Below that nothing of a paragraph, there were a handful of pictures that must have been snapped by the photographer the day before.

What did Stasia have to be sorry about? Em considered calling and asking, but put it off. Em might want to talk to her older sister, and there was no way she was going to confess to that little kiss that she and Andre had shared.

Or not so little. And definitely not little when she thought of his hard length pressed between them.

She rolled to her other side and curled into a ball. Why had she jumped him last night? If she had some sort of magic spell that could send her back in time twelve hours, she would use it.

But with a ghost werewolf prowling the halls, it seemed possible that a spell like that could exist.

No.

She wasn't going to use magic to get out of an embarrassing situation.

Not yet.

It wasn't the stupidest thing she had ever done after a show. That belonged to a night better left unremembered where she was lucky she hadn't been arrested.

Kissing a guy she was supposed to hate—or at

least severely dislike—barely scratched the surface of her antics.

But did she hate him?

There was no question that Andre made her feel things that she would rather ignore. It was like every time he was around, he managed to get right to the heart of whatever she was thinking or feeling. No one had been like that before. Especially not someone that she'd known for a matter of weeks and only spent a handful of hours with.

Because if she ignored the fact that she had climbed all over him and unsuccessfully seduced him the day before, he had been pretty decent. Insistent about canceling the show, which obviously she had not done. And critical of her security staff. And he hadn't watched most of her show.

Okay, maybe he wasn't that great. But at least he hadn't been sniping at her.

But knowing that he was somewhere in her suite kept her plastered to her bed. Also the very soft sheets and plush mattress.

But eventually Em had to face the facts and the man that was waiting for her.

Though it would probably be very easy to protect her if she never left her bedroom again.

That was impossible. The buses would be rolling out in a couple of hours once everything was torn down. Normally she would fly to the next city, but for some reason she was traveling with the buses that day. She didn't question the schedule's intentions, it probably all made sense. At least it would give her more time to talk to her band and go over some of the issues that had come up in the last couple of shows.

With thoughts of work in mind, she was able to force herself out of bed and into something resembling actual clothes. She'd managed to take a shower before passing out, so at least she hadn't slept dirty.

But it would be nice to take a shower right now and stall just a little more.

She seriously considered it, but if she was going to get out of the hotel on time, she really couldn't take the extra time to pamper herself.

Em left her bedroom and followed her nose to where she could smell a bounty of breakfast foods being prepared.

Her suite came with a kitchenette, but she was not much of a cook on the best of days, and this deep into a tour, she was subsisting mostly on junk food and whatever Melinda shoved near her face.

Andre was working the two burners of the kitchenette like he had experience working in a professional kitchen. He had pancakes and eggs and bacon all ready for her once she sat down at the small table.

"Orange juice or coffee?" he asked.

Em wasn't about to question his intentions when she was about to receive a delicious breakfast. "Both, thanks." Sometimes a private chef would prepare meals for her that she could heat up, but they hadn't done that for this city. But it was nice to have Andre cooking for her right there.

She could get used to it.

And then she remembered the rejection of his kiss again and knew there would be no getting used to this. It was a nice morning and she would appreciate it while she had it. But she wasn't going to count on him.

"Was the couch terrible to sleep on?" she asked. The hotel hadn't been able to provide a rollaway bed. The couch folded out into something they called a bed, but she was pretty sure was actually a medieval torture device.

Andre grimaced and brought her drinks before going back and grabbing his own plate. "I've had worse," he said.

"Yeah, but weren't you in the army? Pretty sure a lot of things are worse there."

He shrugged and dug into his food.

He was ignoring the kiss. He didn't look at her like she was anything more than the woman he was protecting. He was being nice, which she could appreciate. But maybe he was just running on some sort of opposite schedule. Most people were grumpy in the morning and got nicer as the day went on. Maybe he started nice and the grumpiness grew by the hour.

It was something to think about.

She was grateful that he wasn't talking about the kiss. For a minute. But she was also pissed. She had taken a real chance there. They could have had a good time. And she definitely would have been willing to sacrifice the prepared breakfast if it meant another kind of morning wake-up call.

Then she took a bite of the bacon and reconsidered. If they could've found a way to mix the sex and also have breakfast, that was what she wanted.

"You can cook," and even she could hear how offensive her tone was.

But Andre just chuckled. "Is that really so surprising?"

It was her turn to shrug.

They didn't talk much during breakfast, but they didn't need to. Andre checked a few things on his phone, and once she was finished, he cleared away the plates.

"So what's the plan for today?" he asked.

Before she could answer, there was a harsh knock on the door. "Thirty minute warning," came Melinda's voice. And then she moved on to the next door, and Em could hear her knocking as she moved down the hall.

"The drill sergeant wants us out. We're heading to the next town." Em chewed faster. The food was good and she didn't want to leave it behind.

"Flight?" Andre asked, and he seemed hopeful.

"No private plane for me." Her family had one, but she wasn't *that* big of a rock star. When she flew, it was either first class or chartered. "We're taking the tour bus."

He just nodded. "Then I'd better go talk with Darlene. Hopefully there isn't an attack while we're in transit."

And he left her alone to deal with packing up her stuff. It was an act she had done thousands of times, and she was usually alone while she did it.

So why when she threw her shirts into her suitcase and carefully packed away her shoes did she feel lonely?

19

THE ARMY HAD nothing on Em's tour when it came to efficiently moving a large group of people. True to the thirty minute warning, they had rolled out in two large tour buses and a handful of semi trucks that contained most of Em's stage.

He hadn't realized just how much they would be taking from town to town.

There were a few hours of travel planned before they would stop for lunch, and then another couple hours before they reached the next city and their hotel for the night. And Andre was hoping the hotel was just as booked as the last one. He didn't want a room of his own. He wanted to be with Em.

He regretted not letting the kiss go further. And if she kissed him again, he didn't think he would hold back. A man only had so much self-control.

But right now, he was content to sit back and watch as she held a meeting with her band. Jerry, Floyd, and Kristin were sitting with her on a couch and two chairs in the middle of the bus. It was more like a motorhome than a bus, designed for comfort on a long drive.

If he concentrated, he could make out the words they were saying over the road noise and the rumbling engine. But Andre let it fade away. He didn't know much about performing music and couldn't tell one chord from another, so when Em gave Jerry a slight rebuke about missing an intro, he wasn't sure what that meant and he knew it wasn't his problem.

If ever he had thought that Em was just some overproduced rock star who didn't care about her craft, watching the meeting blew that assumption out of the water. She was speaking to her band as a musician, not a celebrity. And as they finished up discussing their performances, they shifted over to playing songs that he recognized from the radio but knew were not Em's.

With her safe on the bus, he let his thoughts wander back to the shadow beast. He didn't know if it would attack again now that they had moved on. It was possible that some crazed fan had sent it roaring at her. And though Darlene and Vi had spoken of weird things happening at other stops on the tour, there was no reason to believe they were connected.

Andre wanted an excuse to stay with Em. He didn't want anyone hurt, but if the shadow beast showed itself, then it was evidence that either a crazed fan was following them or something else was causing it to appear.

Someone on the tour? Some sort of charm or totem? At this point Andre was racking his brain for what he had seen in movies and television shows. That was his only touchstone of magic. And he didn't think that episodes of Buffy the Vampire Slayer that he hadn't seen in over a decade were going to help him.

Eventually the bus stopped for lunch. They were at a large truck stop, and Em stayed right around the buses while Melinda and her fleet of assistants met up with one of the people from the restaurant attached to the truck stop to grab large platters full of food. They were far enough away from most of the truckers and commuters that people could not see that Em was with them. But Em didn't seem too concerned. She walked among her crew and smiled and laughed, finally fixing a plate and sitting down to eat her lunch under a tree. Andre got a plate of his own and joined her.

"Afraid the ghost werewolf is going to attack me?" she asked before stuffing a fry into her mouth.

"Shadow beast," Andre corrected.

"What?" It came out muffled around her food.

Andre had to suppress a smile. "Ghost werewolf is a little… I don't like it. Shadow beast. It's a beast. It's made of shadows." At least he thought it was. Shadows and teeth.

"You're changing its name because you want it to sound cooler." She rolled her eyes with a laugh.

Andre felt a bit of heat in his cheeks, but he wouldn't relent. "Shadow beast."

"Shadow beast." She put enough emphasis on it to make it sound just as dumb as ghost werewolf.

"Do you always have meetings like that with your band?" he asked, wondering what tour life was really like for a rock star.

"Jerry's been hounding me for a meeting. We talk. Obviously. And they make me sound good. But I think maybe I've been neglecting them. This is Jerry's second tour with me. The other two are new."

"You don't have the same band all the time?" He'd never thought about it before and didn't know what to expect.

"No. Mercy is a one-woman act. You know, except for the backup band and the backup singers and backup dancers. But those are hired specifically for the tour and when I record an album. I work with a bunch of different people." She looked over at the buses with a faint smile.

"And do you think there's any sort of resentment in the band or the singers? Something that might have them do weird magic shit?" If people changed every tour, it didn't sound like there would be longstanding resentment.

She took a bite of her sandwich and thought, and then she shook her head. "I can't think of why. It's not like I'm any different than a lot of other bands. They know the score. And they're well-compensated."

Andre filed that information away. He didn't know if it was important, but anything could be at this point.

Em's phone buzzed, and she looked at the message. "Melinda is summoning us back. Time to get on the road."

They got to their feet and threw away their disposable plates. Most of the crew and others traveling with them were either on the bus or turned towards it, which explained why no one yelled out to warn them about the beast.

It seemed to materialize out of thin air, and any thoughts that Andre had about it being afraid of the light were gone. The sun shone brightly overhead as the inky black beast charged at them.

Em was a step in front of him, and his heart stopped as he realized the beast was too close for him to protect her. It charged, but instead of attacking her, it went straight through her and swiped its claws at Andre, raking bloody tracks down his arm.

The growl Andre let out sounded weird coming from his human throat, but he used the beast's momentum against it and sent it flying a few feet away from him.

He thought he heard someone call out, but he wasn't sure if it was shock or even if it was a man or a woman. Then there was a bright flash of light, almost like a lightning strike, but that seemed impossible on such a beautiful day, and the shadow beast disappeared.

Andre whipped around, looking to see if the burst of light had come from somewhere or if the beast was regenerating and ready to charge again.

He thought he saw someone move around the back of the bus, but they were too far away and too shadowed for him to make them out.

It wasn't a crazed fan.

But now Andre had to figure out who on Em's tour was trying to hurt her.

20

THE BAND WAS SUPPOSED to be on her bus all the way until the hotel, but Em banished them to the other bus and led Andre all the way back to the largest bunk, sitting him down with a firm press on his uninjured shoulder.

"Stay here," she commanded. She didn't want questions about how he was injured or what had happened. Her mind was whirling with thoughts that the beast had chased them out of the last city, and she only hoped it didn't attack anyone else on her crew. It shouldn't. It hadn't hurt anyone but Andre so far, and she suspected it was only because Andre had fought it.

Why had it gone straight through her? How?

Her hands were shaking as she pulled out her phone and texted Melinda that she would be on the bus alone with Andre and everyone else needed to be on the second bus. That would be a tight fit, but Em refused to feel guilty about it. It would be much worse if someone saw her alone.

There was a pounding on the door, and for a crazy second Em wished that the bus driver would ignore it, but he answered, and she could hear the murmur of voices. Was that Vi? The closer she listened, the more sure she was.

"Jerry wanted me to come get his cell phone, he says he left it here," Vi told the bus driver.

The bus driver's voice was muffled, but a moment later Em heard steps coming down the hallway. She shrank back into the shadow of the small bathroom where she could mostly watch Vi without risk of being seen. True to her word, Vi reached into the cushions of the seat that Jerry had been sitting on and grabbed a cell phone that had fallen by the wayside. She stuck it into her pocket and turned right back around to leave. And it wasn't long after that that the bus door closed and they started up, heading toward their hotel.

Em grabbed the first aid kit and headed back to the bunk. Andre had taken off his shirt and there was a trail of blood leading down his shoulder to his chest.

But it wasn't as bad as it should have been.

Already most of the blood had stopped seeping out of the wound.

Werewolf healing was no joke.

"I'm all right," Andre assured her. He held out a hand for the first aid kit.

But just like the night before, Em felt compelled to help him. That thing had hurt him while trying to come for her. She was responsible for this. She wiped some of the blood away, revealing his newly healed skin, and then she threw away the gauze bandage that she'd used. There was nothing more for her to do.

She was useless when it came to dealing with the shadow beast.

"It wasn't just a crazed fan." She was starting to shake hard as the reality of the situation washed over her. She'd really hoped that they had left their problems behind at the last venue. That was the first place the monster had manifested. But apparently not the last. And there weren't any fans traveling with them.

Well, maybe there was a fan or two at the truck stop, but she didn't think anyone had followed their buses all this way.

"It's a crew member, isn't it?" She looked up at Andre, begging him with her eyes to tell her otherwise.

And Andre's gaze was soft, sympathetic. "That's likely," he confirmed.

She hunched in on herself as if struck. She couldn't exactly call the crew her friends, but they were good people. They seemed to get along. Why would any of them want to hurt her?

Is that what they wanted to do?

"It went right through me." She didn't seem to have much control over what she was saying. Words were just coming out. "It was like a ghost."

"What did it feel like?" he asked.

Em shivered at the memory. "Like static electricity. All my hair stood up on end. I didn't like it."

He reached out an arm and put it around her, tugging her into a hug. Em surrendered to it. She needed contact. Safety. And Andre was the only one who understood what was really going on. He was the only one who had any chance of protecting her at this moment.

"How do we stop it?" she asked. She didn't want any of the crew or her staff getting hurt. For now the beast was fixated on her, but there was no guarantee that it would stay that way forever. What if it turned on them? She knew the damage those claws could do. She had seen it on her clothes, and her bed, and Andre's skin. She shuddered. A human wouldn't be able to heal from that.

"We find out who's controlling it, or what," Andre

said with more confidence that he could possibly be feeling. "Then we go from there."

"You think someone's controlling it?" She'd figured someone had conjured it, but control was a whole other level.

"They must be, right?"

That thought sat uncomfortably in her mind. "Do you think it was really lightning out there?" he asked.

"Lightning?" Her mind was scrambled and reeling, and she had no clue what he was talking about.

"There was a bright flash before it went away."

Em had no idea. She was so far out of her depth she felt like she was free falling. She just wanted this to be over. She didn't want monsters or ghosts or magic interfering with her life.

Slowly some of the fear started to fade away as she sank into Andre's embrace. He propped himself up against a wall, and it was more comfortable sitting against him than it was sitting on the couch. And after several minutes, she found her fingers wandering. He hadn't bothered to put a shirt back on, so she could feel the glorious expanse of naked skin under her fingers.

As she traced the edges of his muscles, Andre let out a contented hum. This wasn't like the night before. He didn't seem eager to get away from her. In fact, he shifted even closer.

She still wanted him. Nothing about the desire had abated since he had appeared. And maybe it should have frightened her, but of all the things that were frightening her now, Andre wasn't one of them.

"Will you let me kiss you this time?" she asked. Maybe he needed a different, gentler, approach. She never would've guessed it of him, but given the way he sucked in a ragged breath, this was what he needed.

"You don't know what you're doing to me," he warned.

"You don't think I feel the same?" It was crazy. Primal. But she no longer wanted to resist.

Andre pulled her close and covered her mouth with his own. The angle was awkward, and Em shifted around until she found herself straddling his legs again and letting him devour her.

The kiss was just as fervent as it had been the night before, but now she knew the difference. Now she had Andre's eager participation. The way he kissed her was almost frightening. But she wasn't going to let go.

Now she had a taste of him. A real, willing taste. And no matter what happened next, she wasn't letting him get away.

ANDRE'S LIPS were imprinted with the memory of Em's kiss as the buses were unloaded and the tide of her tour swept through the new convention center. Just like at the last location, the hotel was connected to the center, and just like at the last location, there weren't enough rooms, so Andre was put into Em's suite.

He wasn't complaining.

And if he played his cards right, he didn't think he would be sleeping on the couch again.

But that was a thought for later. Em had been swept along with the tide. The concert would happen that night, and to get everything ready in a matter of hours, she would be busy until the performance was over.

His wolf insisted he go down and follow her

every step to keep her safe. And Andre would soon. The beast had attacked once that day, and there was no reason to think it couldn't attack a second time. Though he hoped whoever was controlling it needed at least a little time to recharge between attacks.

Andre was betting Em's life and his wolf's sanity that they had at least a couple of hours. And he had to check in with Gibson. Though this wasn't an official assignment, he knew his boss, his alpha, would want an update.

So Andre inspected the room to make sure it was safe and then settled into the chair beside the desk and gave his boss a call. This time, Gibson answered on the first ring. "What's up?"

"Just calling to give the report."

"Yes, we've been reading about it all morning. Should I expect to see you in all of the tabloids this week? Is that part of your strategy to keep your client safe?" Wry humor laced Gibson's words. It wasn't a rebuke. Andre wished it was. The teasing was worse.

But teasing went along with their group dynamic, and he would have to deal with it. "Security is lacking a bit. That photographer should have never gotten up to take that photo."

"So the photo's a complete lie? Just a story to sell to get more clicks?" Gibson didn't sound like he believed it.

But now would be the time to agree with him.

Andre's hand came up and touched his bottom lip. He couldn't deny that there was something between him and Em. He didn't *want* to deny it. What good would denial do when he was already planning on how to get in her bed?

He heard him grumble through the line. "Are you going to say something?"

"Not if I can avoid it." It was the kind of impertinence he never would have dared if they were still in the military, but Gibson wasn't an officer anymore. At least not in Uncle Sam's books.

"Is it the same as Owen?" Now the major was more serious.

Gibson was asking if Em was his mate. And Andre's wolf wanted him to say yes. He wanted to make the claim right then and there. But the man was more cautious. "It's only been a day. How could I know?"

"I think if she wasn't, you would have just denied it. It's not a bad thing. At least it doesn't appear to be." He was understanding. It was Gibson's new mission to discover all there was to know about werewolves, and mating seemed to be part of it.

But Andre had his own concerns. "Our lifestyles aren't exactly compatible."

"All things can be figured out. You've adjusted to our new way of being well enough. And you'll still be part of our family if something changes. If you're no longer working for us."

"No longer working for you? Are you firing me?" This was *not* the way Andre expected this call to go.

And a laugh rumbled out of Gibson. "God no. You keep the kids in line. But I would never force you to choose. So do the job, and don't let us interfere with any sort of decision you might come to."

It was too much to consider, and Andre didn't want to keep talking about it.

Instead, Andre gave a report about the shadow beast, and Gibson said he would do some more research. But when they hung up, Andre was left staring at his phone for several minutes.

He had no intentions of quitting his bodyguard job, even if it had never been his dream in the first place. But Em went on world tours like this every year or so. And if this *thing* between them was something real and not chemistry burning hot and bright and then quickly flaming out, then they would need to find a way to make their lives work together.

But he was getting ahead of himself. Two kisses. He couldn't throw his life away on two kisses. The fact that she had him thinking such things after just one day was perhaps concerning. But his wolf wanted him to go find her.

They'd been apart for long enough.

Andre wanted to go after her as well. But she was

surrounded by people, and so far, the shadow beast had only attacked when he was around and she was otherwise alone. He hoped their luck held.

Because right now it was time for him to hunt the beast and leave his songstress to her work.

22

———

WITH MELINDA DISTRACTED by an issue in the stage set up, Em snuck away to steal a few minutes for herself. The organized chaos of her crew was enough to drive anyone crazy, and she figured they could sort things out without her for a bit.

It wasn't like she was going far. She had a dressing room at this venue just like she did at all of them, and that was where she headed. She had her phone on her too, so it wasn't like no one could get in contact. She knew Andre might throw a fit if he realized that she was sneaking off, but she didn't know where Andre was at the moment, so he didn't get to complain.

The hallways were nearly empty, and of the few people she passed, no one did more than give her polite nod as she made her way to her dressing room.

Em didn't stop them. Everyone was busy and they had a tight turnaround at this location. Getting the concert set up in a couple hours required an act of God, or an amazing act of organizational skills, and Em was content to stay out of the way.

This was the perfect opportunity to grab a cat nap.

And to maybe think about what happened on the bus. She couldn't remember the last time she had been kissed like that. Come to think of it, she was pretty sure she had *never* been kissed like that. And if she and Andre were alone in a room together, she knew they weren't escaping without at least one of them getting off.

Both of them, if she could help it.

It was only by some miracle that they hadn't thrown caution to the wind and had sex on the bus. But Em knew that sound carried, and the presence of the bus driver was enough to keep her pants securely on.

She had a feeling that Andre could make her scream.

Maybe he was avoiding her at the moment. He knew she was busy and couldn't afford a sex break.

And he was probably looking for whatever was causing the shadow beast to appear and attack.

She hoped he figured it out soon.

And a small part of her hoped that he never

figured it out. As long as that danger was there, he was going to be on the tour with her. Once it was taken care of, well, then there was no reason for him to stick around, no reason except the electric heat burning between them.

He had a life back in New York. It wasn't like he was going to give it up for her.

Not that she wanted him to. But she didn't look forward to real life intruding.

Em finally made it back to her dressing room and opened the door. Her nose told her something was weird first, and then her eyes. No one was supposed to be in there.

And yet there was Vi, sitting in front of a scented candle in the dark room, her eyes glowing a strange color.

But that was impossible.

Eyes didn't glow like that.

And shadow beasts didn't stalk the hallways of concert venues or outside of truck stops. She needed to stop relying on what she thought was impossible and start focusing on the things she was seeing.

"What are you doing?" Em demanded. It was probably not the smartest move to confront somebody doing something weird when she was worried that she had a stalker, but she would blame the surprise of the moment.

It wasn't like anyone was going to tell Andre.

"It's not what it looks like." Vi shot up from where she was sitting, and the lights magically came on.

No, not magically. There was a motion sensor which caught Vi's movement.

"Are you doing… magic?" It still felt weird to think about how magic might have been real. It was real. That was the only way to explain the shadow beast. But was Vi the one causing it?

"I didn't do anything wrong," said Vi.

And that just made Em suspect her more.

"Then you have ten seconds to start explaining yourself," said Em with more bravado than she felt. If Vi was some kind of witch, then surely she could use magic. Hopefully she would forget that for the next minute or so.

Vi's shoulders sank, and she held up her hand in front of her face, palm open. There was something sitting in it. Before Em had a chance to figure out what, Vi blew on the substance and it hit Em right in the face.

She got a lung full of it and her eyes burned. She stumbled to the side and sat in the small loveseat that was propped up against the wall. Something weird was going on. Something was happening to her. She had to remember this scene. She had to remember what she was seeing. But unconsciousness was tickling the edge of her mind, and she couldn't hold on as it dragged her down.

Hands on her face woke her up, and it was the ragged snarl from Andre's throat that fully dragged her to wakefulness.

"Em. Em! Wake up!" He shook her shoulders and her head rattled around.

"I'm awake, I'm awake. I must have fallen asleep." Her eyes felt itchy, like pollen was heavy in the air, and she had no idea how long she had napped. She remembered coming to her dressing room to steal a few minutes to herself, but she didn't know how long ago that had been. And Andre certainly hadn't been around when she snuck away. "Why are you so worried? It was just a nap."

Andre's eyes had bled to gold, and she knew his wolf was close to the surface. "I've been trying to wake you up for more than five minutes," he said. "That was no regular nap."

Em looked around the room. It was the same as she had seen it only a few hours ago. There was nothing out of place. "Maybe I was just tired," she reasoned. "Sometimes naps are like that."

"I can smell Vi," he said. "Was she in here?" His eyes glowed golden with the threat of violence.

Vi? Em racked her brain for the last time she'd seen the woman. "I don't think I've seen her all day," she said. "She's probably with the rest of the crew."

Andre breathed deep and leaned in, breathing deeper. "You smell *wrong*," he said. He rubbed his face against her neck, and Em tried not to focus on how good his stubble felt.

"I'm just sweaty," she said.

"That's not it," he said, insistent, his hands roving over her. "I need you to smell like yourself."

Then his lips were on her neck, and Em stopped worrying about what he meant.

23

WRONGNESS SURROUNDED EM; she didn't smell like herself, and Andre's wolf hated it. He clutched her shoulders and breathed deep, trying to identify what was wrong.

She was looking at him like he was crazy, her eyes half-lidded and still a bit drowsy from the nap she claimed she had been taking. But it was a busy day, and he knew Em well enough to know she wouldn't sneak off for a long nap when people needed her.

And Vi's scent was too heavy for him to ignore. She had been in this room. She had done something to Em.

He didn't trust her, and with the shadow beast stalking, he was sure she was a threat.

If Andre was in his right mind, he would run after her and demand to know what she had done. If it had appeared that Em was hurt in any way, nothing could have stopped Andre from attacking the other woman.

But Em wasn't hurt, just a little dazed. And his wolf insisted that he stay there and tend to his…

To Em.

He trailed kisses up her neck and rumbled in satisfaction as his scent covered her and seemed to obliterate the wrongness that was still over every other part of her. She should smell like him all the time, his wolf insisted, and the man couldn't disagree.

"What are you doing?" There was a bit of a laugh in her voice, and one of her fingers splayed through his hair, pulling him close. "Did you remember to lock the door?"

He had no idea. And while he wanted his privacy, there was nothing that could make him take any step away from Em until she smelled right again. "Your scent." He couldn't quite explain it. She had a human nose. She understood some level of his werewolf reality, but he didn't know how he could explain this to a human.

"Is this possessive werewolf bullshit?" she asked, but there was still a smile in her words.

Was this possessiveness? Andre had never been possessive before. All he knew now was that he had a driving need to cover her in his scent so that there would be no mistaking who she belonged... Okay, yes, that was possessiveness.

"Do you want me to stop?" It was torture to ask. And he didn't know how he would get his wolf to agree. Already he could feel the rumblings of resistance.

"We don't have much time," Em warned, still holding on to him. But it wasn't a no.

It wasn't a yes, either.

"Do you want me to stop?" he asked again, even as his hands trailed up her sides, finding a naked line of skin and stroking her until she broke out in goosebumps.

"I'm blaming you if Melinda yells at us." And then she tugged him down onto the small couch.

Yes. Andre had her now. And there was no place he didn't want to kiss, want to touch. He let his hands rove over her and his lips followed. He stripped off her shirt, and it was Em who slipped her bra off and let it drop to the floor.

He looked his fill. Pert breasts with nipples drawn tight, pale skin, and her scent starting to peek through the wrongness as her arousal grew. He wanted her mad with it. Wet and ready for him. But even as Andre's wolf demanded that he claim her for good, he knew that they didn't have enough time. And he knew he was leaving this encounter frustrated.

But only in one way. Because he was going to give Em the pleasure that he didn't have time to take.

His lips closed over her breast and Em arched up into him, the sound she made a primal song of lust. Even when she let herself be lost to it, there was still music in her.

He could love that he knew.

He luxuriated in the taste of her, her skin a silken dream under his tongue. He could imagine what she would be like if they were in bed together, if they had the whole night. And soon they would.

She wouldn't just take then. From the way she was touching him, he knew she was eager to give as well.

But right now, it was Andre's privilege to give this to her.

He wanted her naked, but knew he was being greedy. They didn't have time for full nudity. Not if she was going to give a concert tonight. He let his fingers undo the fly of her too tight jeans and quested until he found her wet heat.

Em moaned again and cried out his name as he found the spot he was looking for, his fingers making tight circles right where she needed it.

"Yes, yes. God yes." Her head lay back against the back of the couch, her hair spread out in a golden halo.

Andre kissed all over her as his fingers continued

to work her sex. He wanted to taste her, wanted her soaking heat around his tongue, but knew if they got that far he wasn't letting her go. Not tonight. Not ever.

Inside his head, his wolf gave a sharp protest at the thought of letting her get too far away. And Andre tried not to think about it. Not when he had her under his fingers.

Not while she was rippling around him and crying out as her climax took her.

Not as he covered her mouth with his own and gave her a searing kiss to remember him by.

She smelled right. She smelled like him. And that was as it should be.

But there was something wrong on the tour, someone still wanted to hurt her.

And Andre was going to do whatever it took to make sure that no one got the chance.

24

Em was off her game. She knew it.

Three songs into her performance and she could already imagine the bad reviews she was destined to receive. She was distracted, caught up remembering the feel of Andre's fingers and lips, and also confused. Not by what she and Andre had done… or, really, what Andre had done to her. But by what had come before that.

Had Vi done something to her?

The production manager spoke forcefully into her earpiece, and Em realized she had missed a cue. Shit.

Jerry played the line again, covering up her mistake, and she shot him a thankful look, but he had a sour look on his face.

She was screwing things up for him, too.

Em began singing and shoved all of her thoughts

into a narrow corner of her mind. She could worry about all that crap later. Much, much later.

She lasted two songs.

Luckily, the audience didn't seem to notice. Critics would. Fans would give her a lot of leeway. At least, she hoped.

She didn't miss a cue, but she did nearly bump into Jerry and heard him say something less than complimentary. Luckily it wasn't loud enough to be picked up by the mics.

She would owe her band an apology after this. Hopefully, they would forgive her.

She figured they would. Everyone had an off night.

Was Vi out there watching her? Was she the person who had summoned the shadow beast?

She didn't know how she had ended up napping in her dressing room. She didn't remember anything before Andre had shown up, and that was the scary part. She should remember. She had a great memory.

So why was there a blank?

The lights went down, and the band put their instruments aside and snuck off stage. This was one of Em's favorite parts of the show, where she really got to show her chops as a singer. No accompaniment, no band, nothing but a spotlight on her and shadows all around.

She lost herself in the song, and it didn't even occur to her to be afraid.

She was halfway through belting her heart out about lost love and finding the strength to carry on when she felt something moving behind her.

At first she thought it was just one of the production crew. They tried to stay off stage during the performance, but sometimes an appearance couldn't be avoided.

But the production crew never caused the hairs on the back of her neck to stand on end.

She didn't turn around and she didn't stop singing. If the beast was lurking in the shadows, she didn't want it to realize that she could sense it. And if it wasn't there, she didn't want to spin around and give in to a paranoid delusion.

She felt breath on the back of her neck. It was no delusion. But it wasn't attacking. It was right there. So close she could reach out and touch it, but it wasn't sinking its gigantic shadowy fangs into her.

What did that mean? Was it trying to protect her?

Or was it trying to terrify her?

Whatever its intent, she was definitely terrified.

What would happen when the song was over? The lights wouldn't come fully back on. It would be brighter, but the stage would still be covered in shadow while her band came back for the next set.

And the spotlight would go off. Not for long. But

with the beast close enough to touch her, any time would be long enough.

Would it attack her then? Was it just waiting for its moment? She knew it wasn't bound to darkness. It had attacked well enough in broad daylight, even if it had been in the shadows of the buses. But she clung to the bright light of the spotlight, careful to keep her hands well within its beam, as if that offered some protection.

She would have to run. There was a microphone stand on the other side of the stage that she could probably use as a weapon if she needed to. Not that weapons did much against monsters made of shadow.

She wanted to run now. Her heart was beating so fast she feared she would collapse and be stuck as petrified prey for the beast. Then again, if that happened, the lights would come on and maybe the beast would disappear.

Em considered it for a second. But she threw the thought away. There was a chance that the production crew would turn off all the lights and try and get her off the stage under the cover of darkness. They would do it in an effort to save her reputation and to obfuscate what had happened. But if that was the choice they made, she was a goner.

Was Andre close? She couldn't see much of anything due to the way the lighting worked. All she had to do was hold the beast off long enough until he appeared. And she was sure he would show up eventually.

Please. Andre. Her thoughts wouldn't do much good, but at least she could hope.

The song was closing out now, her voice reaching higher and higher for that final note. So close. The tremble in her voice wasn't tremolo, it was fear. Wasn't bravado, it was terror.

The beast nudged its nose into the spotlight, testing the edge of her flimsy protection.

Em closed her eyes and took a final breath, ready to run.

The spotlight flicked off, casting the stage in darkness. Em ran for the microphone stand as a second wolf, this one made of fur and flesh rather than shadow, burst onto the stage.

25

ANDRE KNEW he was giving Em's fans a hell of a show, but he didn't care. The beast was out there. It was closer to Em than it had ever been, and he needed to stop it. He charged. It was dark and the fans were so loud he couldn't rely on his sense of hearing. Nor his sense of smell. It was sensory overload from the thousands of people in the crowd, and the shadow beast didn't smell like anything.

Andre knew how to focus even when focus was impossible. Being in a war zone wasn't that different. Bright flashes. Loud noises. The fear that the enemy could get to you any moment.

But right now, he was the one stalking the enemy.

The lights would come up soon. Right now, the audience could only see their shadows moving around. And though it wasn't his priority, Andre did hope he could chase the shadow beast away before it became clear that Em was standing right next to a wolf.

Lightning flashed over his shoulder and Andre flinched. Then he growled.

The audience let out wild screams as another bolt of lightning flashed, and then the shadow beast was running off the stage.

Andre dared a glance behind him and saw Vi standing on the edge of the stage, her hands glowing with the aftereffects of magic.

Was she controlling the beast? Or was she trying to stop it?

Her lips moved, but he couldn't make out what she was saying. It didn't take a fool to understand that she was telling him to go after the beast.

He did.

But by the time he was backstage and prowling the hallways, it was gone. He snuck back to where he had dropped his clothing and shifted back to human, pulling on his clothes and heading back to watch Em finish up her concert.

He could see that she was shaky. How could she not be? But she was one hell of a performer, and she finished the show as strongly as anyone could be expected to after being attacked by a werewolf.

Vi stood backstage, and she gave him an assessing look when he stood right next to her. The band was back on the stage with Em, and no one seemed to realize that something magical happened.

Of course, the lighting guys had to know something was wrong. But they would be looking for electrical faults, not witches.

A witch. That had to be what Vi was, right? But he wasn't going to ask until Em was with him.

The concert finally ended, and it didn't take long for Andre and Em to head back to their hotel room with Vi in tow.

They didn't speak until the door was safely closed.

"What the fuck is going on?" Em demanded.

Vi held up a hand and tilted her head to the side, as if she was listening for something.

"No one's in the hall," Andre assured her. He could hear just fine.

Still, Vi shook her head and then headed to the door, waving her hands in front of it and muttering something until there was a bright flash of light that disappeared quickly.

"Now I'm sure we won't be overheard," she said. She stood up straighter than he'd ever seen, more confident now that she wasn't hiding a part of herself.

"Witches," was all that Em said before she sank down onto the couch in the living area of her suite and buried her face in her hands.

"Witches?" Andre looked at Vi for confirmation.

"Witches." She nodded. "Yes. I'm a witch. Obviously."

"Nothing was obvious about it until you started shooting lightning out of your hands," Em said, her voice still a bit shaky, probably both from the performance and Vi's revelation. She pulled her feet up onto the couch and curled up into a ball.

Andre wanted to go and comfort her, but he also wanted to stay between her and Vi in case Vi got any sort of idea.

"Did you summon that thing?" he demanded. He was almost certain of the answer. He didn't think a person would summon a magical monster only to fight it off. But maybe that had been the whole ploy. Maybe she had summoned the creature just in order to fend it off to ingratiate herself to Em.

"Of course not," said Vi, outraged.

"You're saying a lot of things like we should understand them," said Em. She uncurled herself and sat up straight. "I've never heard of a real witch. You don't exactly look like Sabrina."

"The nineties one or the reboot?" she asked, as if that mattered.

"Neither." Em clearly wasn't happy with jokes.

Vi's shoulders sagged. "I promise I'm not here to hurt you."

"Then why are you here? And you did

something to Em before the show. What was it and why?" Danger was close to the surface, and he wanted to hurt her. But he and Em needed answers more.

Now Vi did look a bit sheepish. "I cast a minor confusion spell on Mercy, I mean, on Em. She caught me in the dressing room scrying for the creature. I didn't think I could explain it. I'm sorry." Her eyes were pleading as she looked at Em. Em just nodded, a bit shell-shocked. Vi kept speaking. "I wanted to work on your crew. I am..." Her cheeks grew red, clashing with her purple hair. "I'm a fan. It seemed fun. And before Mr. Werewolf here showed up, it looked like you needed some protection. I've been trying to figure out where the summon came from, but it's been difficult. Magic is tricky work, and I wasn't exactly expecting to need to perform major spells on this job."

"How did you know I'm a werewolf?" It popped right out of Andre's mouth without him thinking about it.

Both women stared at him, and he remembered how he had transformed and charged the stage. "Stupid question. Did you know before then?"

"Of course. It's obvious." Vi was looking at him like he was a particularly slow student.

"Forgive me," Andre said, words dripping with sarcasm. "I didn't know werewolves were widely identifiable. Or that witches existed." And he didn't like that she could confuse people with her magic.

Vi stared at him in disbelief. "How could you not know that? Your pack doesn't have a relationship with a coven?" Em was forgotten for a moment as she turned to him and gave him a look of grave concern.

"I don't think what my pack has or doesn't have is any of your business," he said. He wasn't sure if he trusted this woman, and he certainly wasn't going to give her more information than she already had.

"So you're saying you're a good witch, right? You confused me a bit with magic, but you didn't hurt me. And you're not going to do it again," Em said, bringing the conversation back to her. "And there's like, a bad witch after me. A warlock?"

Vi rolled her eyes. "Good witch? Bad witch? That's a bit reductive. Witches are just people. Some of us are awesome. Some of us suck. And whoever is after you is definitely of the sucky variety. And now that you know, I have no reason to confuse you again."

Andre wanted to hold Vi accountable, but Em seemed willing to let it go as she spoke. "So what's happening? We thought it was a ghost werewolf at first. Now we're calling it the shadow beast."

"Shadow beast, I like that." Vi nodded, a contemplative smile tugging at her lips. She sat on the table of the room's kitchenette and placed her feet on the chair. "A magic user of some kind summoned it. That much I'm pretty sure. It's not a ghost. It's a spirit or some sort of mental construct. I won't know exactly what it is until I get closer to it. Obviously it can inflict damage, since your mate here seems to be able to attack it. But there are a lot of ways that this thing could have been brought into the world and several ways we can take it out. But we need to work together if we're going to do that."

Andre jolted when she said the word *mate*. He wanted to demand more information. What did she mean by that? Vi potentially had a wealth of knowledge when it came to what it meant to be a werewolf, and she didn't know just how ignorant he was, though she must have had some idea given her tone in this conversation.

"Why is it escalating?" Em asked, shifting a bit where she sat. "At first we were just feeling creeped out. Now it's attacking me."

"Is it?" Vi challenged. "Or is it just lurking and letting itself be seen? As best I can tell, it only fights back when your mate is around."

"You keep saying that word?" Em half asked, half stated, and Andre had trouble deciphering her tone.

"Well, yeah. Isn't he?" She looked between the two of them and pursed her lips. "Or I guess you can figure that out yourself."

Em pushed up from the couch and started pacing.

"So you think it doesn't want to hurt me? It really tore Andre up." She shot him a concerned glance, and Andre smiled back to reassure her.

"You wouldn't fight back when a werewolf is chasing you?"

Neither of them had a response for that. But it did make Andre wonder. "Could whoever is responsible for this be like you? Just trying to protect her from something?" He didn't like the idea of the shadow beast lurking around, but if it was something they didn't need to worry about, he could sleep a bit easier.

Vi shook her head. "He might start off thinking that. But a construct like this is going to take on a life of its own. And before long, it's going to want to do stuff to Em. Perhaps claim her."

Andre couldn't suppress the growl that came from his throat.

Vi nodded in agreement with Andre's wolf. "Not good. I can put protection on your room at night. That will stop it from getting in while you're in here. It will stop anybody from getting in, actually. You stay close to her during the day. I've got some ideas about what could be causing this, but I need to do more research. And now that we're all on the same page, I think we can work together."

"So it's just like that?" Em asked. "Suddenly we're a team? You've been lying to us."

"Would you have believed me if I just walked up to you and told you I was a witch? Performed a couple magic tricks? Come on."

"I accepted werewolves pretty easily," Em said in her own defense, not that Vi could have known that.

"Yeah, but you kind of had no other choice," Andre pointed out. That's what happened when one attacked your sister right in front of you. But he didn't say that part out loud. Vi didn't need to know.

"Do you want my help or not?" Vi asked, arms crossed and toe tapping, as if she was tired of their bullshit.

He and Em shared a look, but the decision was obvious from the start. They knew nothing about magic. Vi seemed to know everything. And they needed the help.

"Yeah, we want your help," Em decided. "Will we be able to get out if you put a protection up on the room?"

Vi nodded. "If no one's in the room, the protection will dissolve. So if you both have to leave, just text me and I can come put it back up. Easiest way around that is that one of you stays in the room if the other person has to go get ice or whatever. Then the person inside can let the other person in and you're good. Nothing can get in without an invitation. Is that good?" She spoke about magic security as if it were as commonplace as an alarm.

"Will you be safe outside the room?" Andre asked. He didn't want their new ally putting herself at risk.

"Oh yeah, I'll definitely be fine." She wasn't concerned at all, and it didn't sound like bravado. "I'll start consulting my sources tonight and see what I can come up with. You two just stay on high alert. Together we can fight this thing."

Then Vi went back to the door and performed some more magic in front of it before leaving the two of them alone in the suite, protected by a spell that neither of them completely understood.

Andre turned around and watched as Em sank back down onto the sofa. "Witches."

It was a lot to take in. But he and his mate were finally alone and safe from the shadow beast for the moment.

His wolf rose to attention within him. It wasn't witches he was thinking about right now.

It was his mate.

26

EM DIDN'T KNOW if her life was falling apart or if everything suddenly made sense. Was it possible for both of those things to be true at the same time? It had to be. Otherwise her brain might explode trying to hold in all the information she'd just learned.

She stared at the door. Vi had done her magic, but no matter how hard Em stared, it just looked like a standard hotel room door. It didn't sparkle with magic and it wasn't surrounded by smoke. Em might have thought Vi was screwing with them if she didn't believe with her whole heart that everything she'd said was true.

Everything.

Even about Andre.

Being her mate.

Mate.

Fuck.

It was a lot to take in. And Andre was several feet away, pointedly not looking at her. Em didn't like that. Everything between them had sprung up way too fast and burned way too hot, but she didn't want to back away.

She was rushing towards a cliff and ready to jump off on the promise that fate would make her sprout wings and fly. It sounded impossible. But so did werewolves and witches, and look where she was now.

"Are you just going to stand there all night?" she asked him. She could move over to him, but it turned out Em was afraid to move too.

"You're taking this well," Andre replied, remaining still.

She could practically feel the energy in the air, ready to explode with something. Would it harm them? Or would it do something she could barely wrap her head around?

It was a bad idea to make decisions in moments like this. Em knew that as well as anyone.

But her mind had been made up ever since the bus. Maybe even before then.

Two days in each other's company.

A month of acquaintance.

And she was more sure of him than people she'd known for years.

Sounded like fate to her.

"She didn't say much that we hadn't already guessed ourselves," and Em thought they deserved recognition for that. Even with little knowledge of magic, they'd managed to figure out the broad strokes of what they were facing.

"She used magic on you." It came out ragged, and Em realized Andre was only holding himself still because he was hanging onto his humanity by a thread.

She took a step closer and saw that his eyes had bled to their wolfish gold. Wolf and man warred for dominance. Another woman might be scared.

But Andre—and his wolf—were hers.

"She didn't hurt me." Em was a bit miffed about the magic, but was willing to let it go. For now. But if Vi did anything like that again, there would be consequences.

"Your scent…" He breathed deeply.

But Em knew there was nothing wrong with it now. "You fixed that. Rather well." Her body burned just thinking about it.

"I can still smell her in this room. Can still remember it." There was a threatening rumble to his voice.

No, not threatening. Full of promise.

Em took a step closer to him and laced their fingers together. "Come with me." She tugged him toward the bedroom. "Is her scent in here?" Em smelled nothing but the clean room, but Andre was the werewolf and he had the better nose.

He shook his head.

"Do you want to make sure?" she asked, her own voice going husky.

That was all the encouragement he needed. He tugged her close, burying his fingers in her hair as he crushed their mouths together in a searing kiss that lit Em up from the inside.

Her clothes were too tight. The room was too hot. Her legs were weak.

And it was perfect.

And it only got better as Andre's tongue swiped against hers and claimed her, imprinting his taste on her for good. It was the kind of kiss that took a person over, that made them know there was no going back. The kind of kiss that could be terrifying.

But the promise of it was exactly what Em wanted, what she needed. Nothing in her life was certain. And everything she'd once known was true no longer held. But she had Andre, and whatever force was pulling them together was more than right.

She tore at his shirt, probably *would* have actually torn it if she was just a bit stronger, but it was cue enough for Andre to pull it off and leave all those rippling muscles on display for her. She wanted to look her fill, but she wanted to kiss him more.

Kiss him she did. She kissed him until her jaw ached, and even then the discomfort was washed away on a wave of pleasure as his hands quested low.

Where had her own clothes gone?

One moment she was sure she was fully clothed, and then Andre seemed to weave his seductive spell and she was lying naked on the bed. This wasn't actual magic. They didn't need magic. Not outside what they could produce between their two bodies.

Andre took the rest of his clothes off and came down on her, kissing her again. She couldn't get enough of his lips. There was something joyous in it, like they were sharing a new discovery with one another, one she wanted to study for the rest of her life.

She knew it was too fast, but nothing in Em could regret it, not when his kisses made her heart speed up and think thoughts about forever.

She could learn everything about what Andre liked if they had forever. Already she could feel the way his body responded when she ran her hand up his left side, fingers trailing over his spectacular ass. What other spots would make him moan? She wanted to taste every inch of him and then some. She wanted to ride him and watch him as he came.

But it was Andre who trailed kisses down her body and began his own study of what made her shiver. And then his head was between her legs, and Em believed he really was a sorcerer from the spell he cast over her.

Her fingers curled into the sheets, and she couldn't help the hoarse cry that tore from her throat, urging him on. He seemed to know exactly what made her desperate for more, and Em didn't know if it was his special talent or some sort of mystical werewolf magic.

She didn't care, so long as he didn't stop.

He didn't. He gave her more, his body worshiping her with his tongue and his hands. And when he had wrung every ounce of pleasure she thought she could give, she crested and came, calling out his name.

But Andre wasn't done.

And she could love him for that.

He kissed her again, wet and filthy and everything she wanted. And then he was at her entrance, his cock teasing her and making her beg.

He made her want to sing.

He thrust into her and Em moaned, clinging to him as her body pulled him further in. The fit was tight and perfect as her body adjusted.

They moved together. Em had waited an eternity for this moment with Andre, no matter how quickly attraction had flared between them. She couldn't pull away from it now, nothing in her wanted to.

This was where she was meant to be, who she was meant to be with.

And as her body surrendered and shuddered against his, she knew there was no going back.

There were words to say, but it was much too soon, so she said it with her body and her kisses instead. And if she was brave, she would think that Andre was telling her the exact same thing.

But Em wasn't brave enough to speak, and she'd already been asked to believe the impossible once today.

She let sensation take her, and when she came for a second time, she wished that it would always be like this.

Her and Andre. Together.

27

EM RESTED EASILY, but morning came quickly and Andre couldn't sleep anymore. They were wrapped all around each other in the bed, and he looked at her for a long while, paying attention to the curve of her jaw and the way her blonde hair fanned out over the pillow exactly as he imagined it.

This was the kind of heaven he had never dared to dream of. And if he wasn't careful, it would all slip through his fingers before he could make it his for good. He didn't want to think it, and he wouldn't let those thoughts stain their bed.

Andre slipped away, careful not to wake Em from her dreams. She worked hard and she needed the rest, especially considering how late they had stayed up the night before.

He had to turn away, to convince himself that

kissing her awake and renewing their lovemaking was *not* the way to start the day.

They could do that after she woke up later.

But first he needed to truly consider all that he had learned the night before. He and his pack knew that magic must exist. After all, a witch, or a warlock, or a wizard of some kind had performed a spell on them in the Black Forest of Germany nearly three years before. None of them had been bitten, none of them had known what was happening.

And then one night, more than a month later, they transformed and ran through the woods as wolves.

He and the others had been stumbling through their lives ever since then. After the abduction but before the first transformation, they had all been kicked out of the military, given large payouts for their silence. Andre didn't think the military knew exactly what had happened to them. They had been dismissed to prevent an international incident with one of the country's strongest allies.

He and his pack were lucky. He shuddered to think what would've happened if they had become wolves when the military still owned them. Tests. Secret detainment facilities. A whole lot of needles. And no hope of freedom over again.

But Vi's information now gave him more than any of them had learned up to this point. They had been stumbling through, figuring out the limitations of their abilities by trial and error. But there was no way to test magic, not when none of them knew a thing about it.

Though he had seen Rowe perform a few card tricks that bordered on sorcery, not that it counted for anything.

Somehow, he was pretty sure that Vi would tell him it wasn't the same.

And then there was the mate thing.

Andre's wolf perked up at that thought. And it wanted to insist that he should go back into the bedroom and wake Em up to claim her. There had been a point the night before where he had been almost certain that he should grow fangs and bury them in her skin, marking her as his mate for anyone to see.

He had resisted. Barely.

And he could not let his wolf rise to the surface, or he knew he would not be able to resist again.

He didn't know the full extent of what mating meant for wolves. Was it fate? Chemistry? Owen and Stasia were feeling out their own relationship, and Andre had not felt the need to pester them to try and figure things out.

But now he needed to know. Now he had Em. And he was determined to be the best mate that he could be.

Did she want that? They had gone from barely

tolerating one another to bed in a matter of days, and while he knew his heart, he didn't know hers. Would she expect him to walk away when this was all done?

His wolf didn't like that, and he didn't either. He wasn't sure that he *could*. But it was a problem for later. He had to keep her body safe before he could claim her heart.

And hopefully he would have time to ask Vi more questions about what it meant to be a wolf, what it meant to be a mate, and about everything there was to know about magic.

Andre had a long list of notes and questions, but he knew Gibson would be happy to receive them. It was more intelligence than they'd had in a very long time. And it might finally start to unravel the mystery of what they were and why they had been turned.

Andre didn't really care about the why. He was inclined to think they had been convenient targets, as convenient of targets as people living on a secure military base could ever be. Or maybe it was their military training that made them ideal.

There was nothing special about him. His family was as normal as they came, and before he'd been turned into a werewolf. he couldn't fool himself into thinking he had been anything spectacular.

A bit broody. A bit inclined to sulking. But not the

kind of person that was destined to become a werewolf.

He didn't care about destiny. It had never done anything for him. Except maybe put him in Em's path.

And he would thank it for that. But *only* for that.

He looked over his notes again. He would need to rewrite them and put them into a more coherent order before sending them on to Gibson.

But he could hear Em moving around in the bedroom, and he put the notebook aside. It could wait for a bit. He wanted to wish his mate a good morning.

2 8

———————

It was the perfect morning. As long as Em could ignore thoughts of the shadow beast and witchcraft and all of the bad things that were happening. She had Andre in her bed and a clear schedule until well after noon.

She wanted to take advantage of it, both in the sheets and out of them. Her body was sated, but her heart wanted more.

When she suggested that she and Andre go out on a breakfast date, she wasn't actually worried he would say no. But his yes untightened something she hadn't realized was tight in her chest.

There weren't any paparazzi waiting as they left the hotel and grabbed a cab to take them downtown to one of the restaurants that had been recommended to her. On the ride she could pretend that she was just a normal woman sitting next to a normal man going out for a bite to eat after a spectacular night together.

She wasn't a rock star. Andre wasn't a werewolf. And there wasn't a magical beast after her.

But she *was* a rock star, and Andre *was* a werewolf, and the beast could attack her at any minute.

Her shoulders sagged as reality threatened to intrude.

Andre reached out and laced their fingers together. "You okay?" he asked.

"Did your fancy werewolf powers tell you something?" And then she could have cursed herself for saying werewolf. They were speaking quietly and the taxi driver's music was loud, but that didn't mean that he couldn't hear them. Hopefully he would assume he'd misheard. It was just the kind of story she didn't need showing up in the tabloids.

"You just looked nervous," Andre assured her, giving her hand a squeeze, his eyes bright and caring.

"A lot is going on." It was barely a summation, but it wasn't like he didn't know. They both needed this little break. Vi would no doubt come and try and find them soon enough. But they could just have a few hours together to be normal.

The restaurant didn't have a back room or any

particularly secluded tables, but Em decided it was worth the risk. It was a little American bistro that specialized in fancy brunch and was beloved by half of Instagram.

She would commit a lot of sin for waffles that looked as good as the pictures she had seen online.

Conversation between the two of them was easy, easier than she had ever expected. Andre broke the ice by telling her a funny story of some of the shenanigans that Owen and Stasia had gotten up to in the last month, one of which inexplicably involved a water slide and a lot of bubbles.

She couldn't shoot back with any information about their mutual friends, but a laugh burst out of him when she detailed a prank that some of the road crew had played on her at the first tour stop.

Their food had not been served by the time a few patrons started taking surreptitious cell phone photos of the two of them. Em wanted to grimace. The paparazzi didn't need to know where she was when there were plenty of regular people eager to invade her privacy.

But she couldn't show her frustration. That only made the pictures worth more. And then there would be a story about how she was impolite to a fan or how she was a diva or how she was doing this all to herself.

"Can I hold your hand?" Andre asked quietly,

shooting a glance over her shoulder and probably looking at one of the many cameras that was not subtle. "How do you want to play this?"

He wasn't trying to suck up the attention, which was good, and even better, he didn't seem weirded out by it. Em had run into both of those problems before. Either people dated her because they wanted their picture on blogs and social media and in the tabloids, or they couldn't stand the attention and ran away before anything could get serious.

Andre wasn't running.

Of course, this kind of crap wasn't nearly as weird as the shit he had been dealt.

She reached out and clasped his hand. Rumors were already starting, and if he stuck around, she might need to make a statement. What would the world think of her werewolf boyfriend?

Was that what he was? She wanted to ask. She also never wanted to say the words. A month ago, she didn't know that werewolves existed, and now she was sleeping with one. Now she had a witch and a werewolf protecting her from some sort of shadowy ghost werewolf that was trying to attack her on tour.

Her life was way too weird to start freaking out about something as simple as liking a guy, but she feared that if they went much further in their nascent relationship, everything she was feeling would be much more than *like* very soon.

She didn't fall hard and fast. That never happened.

But maybe it never happened because none of the people she had been with before were Andre.

"You're looking serious," Andre said, running his thumb over her hand and sending shivers up her arm.

"Just thinking," she said with a safe smile; she didn't know what she was ready to reveal just yet.

"Want to share?"

She might have if the server hadn't come with plates laden with food. She wasn't sure how Andre could eat so much, but apparently werewolves had magic metabolism and she would just look on in horrified wonder as he ate two full breakfasts.

Her stack of waffles was just as delicious as it looked on Instagram, and maybe she wouldn't be spending so much time watching Andre eat while she could take her time scarfing down her food.

She put the people and their cell phone cameras out of her mind. She was eating breakfast with a friend. Maybe a boyfriend. So what?

It wasn't really that interesting, and she wasn't about to give them a story.

Instead she was determined to enjoy her morning with Andre.

After their food was done, they waited around and had an extra cup of coffee. And after that, they took a walk. The city they were in had a beautiful park downtown with a walking path heavily shaded by trees that muffled the city sounds and let them imagine they were in a place free of all the annoyances of modern life.

She and Andre held hands as they walked and it was nice.

So nice that she feared getting used to it. If she got used to it, her heart could be broken. Once the shadow beast was gone, Andre wouldn't have an excuse to stick around. Not unless she took a chance and asked him to stay, as scary as that thought was.

She had a feeling Andre might be worth the risk.

But eventually their morning had to come to an end. She was expected back for an interview in less than an hour and needed to get ready. And Andre probably needed to talk to Vi so they could come up with a plan to defend Em while she walked on stage and sang her heart out.

They hailed a taxi to head back to the hotel, and before she and Andre could start talking, her phone rang, the ID indicating it was from her manager.

"Hey, what's up?" She didn't get many managerial calls, especially when they weren't in contract negotiations, planning a tour, or planning an album.

"Do I need to get PR people on this?" her manager demanded.

"On what?" For a horrifying second, she wondered if the shadow beast had shown up in fan photos.

But her manager didn't say anything about that. "This guy you're with. What's that all about? You know I need to know if you're about to start dating someone."

Em burst out laughing.

"What's so funny?" her manager demanded.

But Em couldn't come up with a coherent response. She managed to gasp out a promise to call her manager back and then shut the ringer off of her phone and stuck it back in her pocket. It was such a mundane problem that Em couldn't wrap her mind around it.

She wished the biggest issue was that the world was going to find out about her boyfriend sooner than she was ready to tell them.

She would take that over a ghost werewolf any day.

THAT NIGHT'S concert felt a bit different than the others that Andre had been present for. For starters, he was getting more and more looks from the crew as they wondered who exactly he was to Em. The pictures from that morning had only added more fuel to that fire, but he wasn't going to worry about that yet. His own pack had already sent him half a dozen text messages full of emojis, gifs, and jokes that he would have cursed at if he had been with them rather than communicating via text.

Rowe had given him a call and asked what the real reason was that Andre didn't want backup. Andre had only growled.

But it was all in good fun. If he came back from this job mated to Em, then he knew that the pack would accept her. A lack of acceptance wouldn't have stopped him, but it was one obstacle he didn't have to worry about.

He had to put all of that out of mind. The real reason that tonight felt different than the others was that he had some idea of what he was looking for and an ally in Vi. They had split up their duties for the start of the show and planned to swap roles halfway through. For now, Andre was watching Em and the rest of her band perform the songs that had made her a star. Just as she had suggested, he had found some earplugs, and they made it much more bearable to stand so close to the speakers.

He didn't like that he was cutting off one of his senses, but given the drone of the speakers, it was a necessity. And the more times he attended these concerts, the more he got used to the sensory overload.

His wolf didn't like it. His wolf would have to suck it up.

Halfway through the show, Vi came up and stood beside him as they watched Em finish one of her numbers. This was where they'd had trouble last time. The band shuffled off the stage, and he saw the guitarist be hailed by one of the backup singers and pulled into conversation when he looked like he was about to sneak away to the bathroom or something. The lights went down, and Andre's senses went on high alert.

Was the beast out there waiting to attack Em?

Was it stalking the shadows?

He didn't sense anything.

There was a dull hum coming from Vi, and pretty quickly Andre realized it was magic. She was using those senses to figure out if the beast was out there.

Andre was ready to spring into action. This time he would attack as a man, not a wolf. That was, if he needed to.

The spotlight tracked Em as she walked across the stage, and she gave no indication that she was afraid of a magical attack.

The song came to a close, and the lights went out for a moment while the band rushed back on stage. And then the lights came back on and they went into the next song.

"I didn't sense anything," Vi said. She was looking around backstage as if trying to figure out the variable that had stopped an attack.

"Me neither," Andre replied, uncomfortable with the dissatisfaction running through him. "But is that so weird? Maybe whoever did it just had the opportunity last time. An opportunity they didn't have now."

Vi considered it with pursed lips and a raised eyebrow. "I've got the main stage now. I didn't find anything backstage. Maybe your nose will be more helpful."

Andre left her to it. According to Vi, whoever was controlling the shadow beast would need an altar or something like that to channel their power. And since they were assuming that whoever was behind the attacks was a member of the crew, they were also assuming that the altar would be somewhere backstage.

Andre pictured something huge made of obsidian and covered in melting red wax candles. Luckily, Vi had told him what to look for. It was more likely to be something small, something portable that the assailant could set up in a matter of minutes.

Vi had used her magic senses to try and find it, but now Andre would use his nose. All he knew was that the shadow beast didn't smell like anything. So he was on the lookout for an absence of scent. It was a strange thing to look for, but it was all Andre had to go on.

He started close to the stage and tried not to look suspicious. There were all manner of crew working to make sure that the show went off without a hitch. He had to stay out of their way before they started to think that he was causing some kind of trouble.

He worked down one hallway and then another, testing doors and finding utility closets and dressing rooms, all of which seemed to be used for their normal purpose.

He thought he was onto something on his third

utility closet, but the sounds he heard coming from inside it were two crew members stealing an intimate moment, and he decided not to open the door.

They didn't need to be caught, and he didn't need to see two strangers fucking.

His nose didn't tell him anything, and eventually he returned backstage no more successful than Vi had been.

"No luck?" she asked.

Andre just shook his head.

"Maybe you freaked him out last time. Maybe he didn't expect his construct to be attacked."

"Or maybe he's just too busy tonight. Can you do more…" Andre glanced around at the people near them, "of your stuff and see if you can figure anything out?"

Vi splayed her fingers out, and they glowed faintly in an unnecessary show of magic. "Already planning to. I say we take this as a good sign for now. I'll put up the same protections on your suite tonight. Just be happy you have the breather."

Andre couldn't be happy. He didn't think this was a breather. This was the calm before the storm.

30

A WEEK and a half went by, and as they rolled into Chicago, Em really wanted to believe that the shadow beast was gone. There had been no attacks since that night on the stage, and neither Andre nor Vi had managed to catch sight or magical signature of the monster.

That should have made Em happy. She didn't exactly *want* to be attacked by a magical creature. But if they determined it was truly gone, then maybe Andre would go away too.

She didn't want that at all.

Over the past week and a half, she and Andre had grown closer and closer. They couldn't keep their hands off one another, and there had been more than one occasion where someone almost walked in on them in a compromising position while they were making out in her dressing room.

It wasn't her fault that his lap was so comfortable. Especially when it came to kissing him.

Luckily, no press had managed to sneak back and take compromising photos.

She didn't know what the mate bond was supposed to feel like. Vi hadn't given any more information, and Stasia hadn't wanted to say much about it any time Em had asked.

The mate bond didn't matter as far as she was concerned. Her feelings were real. And intense.

Was that a good thing? She wasn't sure how she was supposed to think about fate pulling her to another person. But it didn't feel like some otherworldly force was controlling her relationship. As a matter of fact, nothing had ever been more natural than what she felt with Andre.

And she didn't want him walking away once they were sure the shadow beast was gone.

She also didn't know if she could ask him to stay. He had a job back in New York. She still had months on this tour. If they admitted what they were becoming to one another, how would it survive if they both had to walk away for months at a time?

Other couples handled long-distance just fine. And she knew she could handle short separations. She was a full-grown woman with a life of her own.

She didn't need Andre with her every hour of the day.

But a matter of weeks was different than a matter of months.

She was getting ahead of herself. They hadn't discussed emotions. There had been loaded looks and intense kisses. And she would never forget what it felt like to have Andre inside of her.

But they hadn't said anything about the future.

She supposed that Andre could just be with her because it was convenient. Their attraction sizzled hot and burned bright. If they walked away from one another, it might burn out.

But Em didn't think that was the case. They weren't a wildfire burning through the forest and city that would eventually burn to embers. They were more like the sun, a ball of fire that would take billions of years to extinguish.

And even then, she still doubted that they would ever be doused.

It was fast, and intense. Too much to really consider. But she couldn't do anything but consider it when Andre was around her all the time.

They had snuck away for a little while and were napping after their afternoon lovemaking for the moment. It was so perfect that Em wanted to capture this moment in time so she never forgot it.

Andre's lips brushed against her stomach, and he

looked up at her from where he was laying with his head in her lap. "Weren't you supposed to be sleeping?" he asked, his voice husky and intimate.

"You think that was enough to tire me out?" she teased, her smile growing wider as desire darkened Andre's eyes.

"I'll show you exhaustion," he half threatened, half promised.

Em leaned down and kissed him.

A sweaty half hour later, Andre sat up from the bed, his body radiating satisfaction. "I need to go and patrol before your show. The beast might be lurking."

She wanted to entice him to stay for a few more hours. Or at least *an* hour. Eventually Darlene was going to come looking for her, or Melinda or anyone else that had some sort of pull on her time. But she also didn't mention that the beast hadn't attacked in over a week. Andre knew it as well as she did. And talking about it might break the spell of what was going on between them.

"Stay safe," she told him as he pulled on his clothes and got ready for battle.

Andre leaned down and gave her a thorough kiss. "That's your job. Let me make sure you stay safe."

"I guess that's why you're here." She didn't mean to say it. She didn't want to have this conversation yet.

And she couldn't read the look that passed over Andre's face.

He kissed her again, even harder this time. If she was brave, she could read something into what she was feeling from the kiss. She could imagine that Andre was trying to tell her something. But he pulled back and didn't say anything.

"Give Vi a call and have her put the protections back up on the room if you're going to stay in here for a while. Otherwise, I'll see you backstage."

He took off, and Em sunk back down onto the bed.

She heard the door open and close as Andre left her alone, and she looked over at the bedside table where her phone was sitting so innocuously. He was right. She should give Vi a call. Mostly Vi only put up the protections around her and Andre's suite when they were in for the night. The protections fell every morning when both of them left the room. And since she and Andre had snuck back up to their room for their afternoon delight, it meant they had been sitting unprotected.

Not completely unprotected. She always felt safe when Andre was around.

But he wasn't there anymore.

She reached for the phone and groaned when she saw that her battery was dead.

Stupid. Stupid. But she and Andre had gone to

bed the moment the door closed behind them the night before. And she had been a bit distracted and had forgotten to plug her phone in.

And then she had left it behind that morning. She didn't need people bugging her.

Em scrambled out of bed and found her charger and plugged the phone in. She had a portable charger somewhere, and she would need to take it down to her dressing room, but at least she had time to take a shower. She would probably be safe enough.

And what Andre didn't know wouldn't make him worry.

She let the water soak into her bones in the shower. The hot spray was the second-best feeling she'd had all day. And she took more time than necessary.

But eventually she had to go out and start getting ready for the show that night.

She was half dressed when she heard something clatter to the floor in the other room.

"Andre?" she called out. He usually wasn't so clumsy, but he was the only person with the key to her room.

He didn't call back, and a bit of apprehension sizzled through her.

Em crept towards her phone and was thankful to

see that it had enough battery so she could give Vi a call.

Something else clattered in the other room, and Em did not call out again. That wasn't Andre.

Either a person was in the suite, or it was the shadow beast. She turned on all of the lights in the bedroom and locked the door, as if that would do something to keep a magical construct out.

Then she dialed Vi's number.

But before she could say a word, the beast burst through the door like a ghost moving through walls, and pain ripped through her as it attacked.

31

IN THE HALLWAY, Andre ran into Em's guitarist, one of the backup singers, and a crew member getting out of the elevator. He realized he probably needed to start learning names if he was going to stick around.

They exchanged polite nods, and then Andre got into the elevator and headed down to the ground floor. He considered giving Vi a call. He didn't like leaving Em alone in the room without the protection spell up, but he had mentioned it to Em and he had to trust her.

Besides, it had been a week and a half since any sort of attack. Maybe the beast was scared off by his and Vi's teaming up. Maybe the beast was gone.

Or maybe it was biding its time.

Andre wasn't convinced that it was gone. And it

wasn't just because he wanted to cling to a reason to stay at Em's side.

Unease began to suffuse him as he continued heading toward the concert venue. He wanted to turn around and run back to Em. His wolf jerked at him so hard that Andre had to stop walking for a second. It insisted that something was wrong with his mate.

But Em wasn't his mate. Not yet. He hadn't claimed her. And he still hadn't asked Vi what mating really meant.

But Em would be his. If she allowed it.

He continued on. He wanted to get a feel for this venue before the show later that night. It was best to do that while things were still getting set up. But Andre's wolf was still uneasy.

He tried to convince it that he would see Em later and that all would be fine.

His wolf didn't believe him.

It was only a few minutes later that Andre felt like claws were being raked across his chest, and it startled a gasp out of him. He looked down, his hand traveling to capture all the blood that wasn't falling from him.

He wasn't the one that was hurt.

Em.

He wasn't psychic. He was just a regular werewolf, whatever that meant. But he was certain that Em was in danger and he needed to get to her.

Andre took off running back towards the room. A few of the crew members yelled after him, but Andre ignored them.

He punched the button several times to call the elevator, and it seemed to be taking forever. With a curse, Andre ran for the stairwell and made his way up the old-fashioned way. He wasn't even out of breath by the time he made it to the fourteenth floor. He burst into the hallway ready to face any threat, but there was nothing out of place. No one was there on the verge of attack.

He sprinted the rest of the way to the room and was shocked to find Vi standing outside, her hands glowing with magic as she tried to use her powers to unlock the door.

Andres hands were shaking as he pulled out his key card and unlocked it for her. He didn't ask why she was there. Maybe it was some magical sense. Maybe something had happened while Em called her to reset the spell.

But it was bad. Andre knew it was bad.

As soon as the door was open, the metallic scent of blood assaulted his senses. He found Em on the ground in the bedroom, a dark red pool of blood all around her, soaking into her once white towel and making it red. She was deathly pale, and her blonde hair now looked auburn from all the blood that surrounded it.

She was still gasping and Andre clasped her hand, unsure of where else to touch her. She was on the edge of death, he could tell. And he could smell no scent except for her own blood. It was a sure sign that the beast had been the one to attack.

He looked up at Vi. "Can you fix her? Do some magic?" He didn't know what sort of magic Vi was capable of, but it was all that he could think that might save Em.

No ambulance would get there in time. No hospital was close enough.

Vi had lost her color, and her mouth opened and closed several times as if she could not get the words out. She looked like she was about to throw up.

"Get a hold of yourself," Andre commanded in the same voice he would have used on a new recruit. "She needs you."

"I can't," Vi gasped out. "I'm not a healer. I don't —" She crumpled to her knees. But she wasn't out. She took two steadying breaths, not that there was much that would do when the room smelled so much like blood.

Andre's wolf whined in his head. This couldn't be how it ended. He would never forgive himself if she died because he had left her alone for ten minutes.

"You can save her," said Vi, reaching out and clutching his arm. "Maybe. I hope."

"How?" If she was going to summon a devil right now and have him make a deal, he would do it in a heartbeat.

But that wasn't what Vi was proposing. Some of her composure seemed to come back. "If you turn her into a werewolf, her wounds should heal. Maybe. I can speed up the change with my magic. It's our only shot."

It would work. It had to work. But just before Andre shifted, he ran his hand over Em's cheek. She didn't get to make this choice. And he didn't want her to regret it. "Em, Em. Wake up."

She moaned, and the sound broke his heart. But her eyes fluttered open. They were still full of life and pain.

"I can help you," Andre said. "But you're going to be like me. Is that what you want?" He didn't know what he would do, how he would survive if she said no.

Em blinked her eyes twice and then lost consciousness again.

It wasn't a no.

He didn't let himself think about how it wasn't a yes either.

Andre stripped quickly and changed into a wolf faster than he ever had in his life.

He knew it didn't matter where he bit her. And he didn't want to cause her more pain. So he tugged on her arm gently and felt his fangs break the skin.

His hackles rose as Vi began to perform her magic, and Andre didn't pull away. This had to work.

Eventually the magic grew too strong and Andre backed up, shifting back to his human form without a conscious thought.

He stared at Em's wounds, watching for the sign that they were beginning to close, that she was healing.

He couldn't be sure. And the scent of blood around him was disorienting.

Then Em's eyes snapped open and she screamed.

THE PAIN that ripped through Em was unlike anything she had ever experienced before. Her blood was on fire with it, and she would do just about anything to make it stop. And then she felt light sink into her veins and chase the fire away.

The reprieve didn't last long. Her bones crunched and reformed, and her mind whited out, unable to handle whatever was happening to her.

She drifted. It could have been a minute or a month, but eventually she felt a familiar presence at her side.

Andre. His fingers stroked through her fur, and she heard him murmuring words of encouragement, though she couldn't quite make out what he was trying to say.

Wait. Her fur?

Em tried to stand, but when she tried to push herself up onto her legs, she discovered that she had four instead of two and fell back to the ground, letting out a short bark of frustration.

Fur.

Bark.

What was going on?

She tried to speak, but it came out as a whine instead. The room smelled weird. No. Not weird. It just smelled more. More than she had been able to smell when she had just been human.

Because it was becoming abundantly clear that she wasn't human anymore.

Was this a dream? A nightmare? It felt more real than just about anything.

She recognized Andre's scent immediately, and it calmed her like nothing else. There was another scent too. Kind of smoky and cut through with electricity. Vi. The witch.

Andre kept petting her and it felt good, but his words didn't mean anything to her ears. She didn't know if that was a werewolf thing or if that was a her thing. But she wanted to be human again. She wanted to know what he was saying.

She strained her muscles and reared up onto her hind legs, trying to force herself to change back to human.

It didn't exactly work.

But Andre helped her back to her feet and got very close to her, and this time his words started to make a little sense.

"Focus on yourself," he said, his words still sounding like they were coming from far away even as the sounds were almost too loud for her extra sensitive ears. "Picture it. Hold your human body in your mind and bring it out. You can do it."

That was easier said than done when his intoxicating scent was right there. And Em would have words for him when this was over.

But she knew what she looked like. She knew who she was. And she could summon those ideas with a thought.

At least, theoretically she could.

She thought she was doing it at first, but then something inside of her cracked, and Em lost focus on what she was trying to do at the sharp stab of pain.

Did it hurt every time? She wanted to ask Andre. But she couldn't do that until she had human vocal cords. All she could manage was a canine whine.

She tried again. She was expecting the first crack of bone when it came, but then something snapped right after it.

If Em could have said anything, she would've been cursing a blue streak.

And when Andre made encouraging sounds, she

snapped her teeth at him. She didn't want gentle encouragement right now. She wanted this to be over.

Em dragged a deep breath in through her wolfy snout and went for it, ignoring all of the pain. It was like doing a rehearsal after hours and hours of practice, her feet nearly bleeding and her lungs ready to give out from exertion. But she needed to finish the rehearsal, and this time she needed to finish the change.

It took time. She wasn't sure how much, but eventually she was naked and human and sitting in Andre's lap.

She didn't care that Vi was right there looking at her. And it ended up being a good thing a moment later when Vi handed her a soft blanket that she could wrap around herself.

"You're okay, you're okay." Andre had his arms wrapped tight around her, and he kept saying it, repeating it more to himself than for her benefit.

Em was alive. But she wasn't certain that she was okay.

"What's going on? What happened?"

Andre's arms tightened around her. "The beast attacked you. What we did was the only way to save you." He sounded worried, like she was about to push him away because he had changed her into a werewolf.

An inappropriate laugh burst out of Em. It was like a dam bursting. Was she supposed to get angry at Andre for saving her life? The werewolf thing would take some getting used to, that was certain. But her sister had taken to it like it was nothing, and Em wasn't about to let Stasia upstage her. "We'll deal with the werewolf thing later," she said. "The beast attacked me? How?"

"The protections weren't up over your room," said Vi, and there was a hint of censure in her voice. "It must have taken the opportunity."

And that was Em's fault. She should've called Vi immediately after Andre left the room. Now that she was conscious again, she was remembering everything that had happened. "How long has it been?" She reached out her hand, and her fingers landed in something sticky. Her new werewolf nose knew exactly what it was before she picked up her fingers and looked at the red liquid clinging to them.

Blood.

Her blood.

"Two hours," said Andre. "He attacked you two hours ago. I told Melinda you had food poisoning. The concert tonight is canceled."

Em whipped around to look at him. "What? No! I have to go on." She tried to get out of his embrace, but even that tiny struggle had her limbs shaking with exhaustion. She could barely stand. There was no way she could perform.

"You almost died," Andre shot back. And he sounded so vulnerable that Em had to wrap her arm around him and give him back some of the comfort he was giving her.

"But I didn't. And maybe you're right about the concert. For tonight."

Andre kissed her cheek. And if Vi wasn't right there, she would have shown him exactly how grateful she was for him saving her life.

Em looked over at the witch and narrowed her eyes at the woman's calculating expression. "What are you thinking?"

Vi grinned. "I have an idea on how we can stop the shadow beast."

33

Em was ready to attack the shadow beast right now. No waiting. Just running straight into danger. Unfortunately, Vi still had some preparations she needed to make before they could make their move. She left Em and Andre alone in their room with the protections now up and an assurance that the shadow beast couldn't get to them.

Em looked back at the pool of blood on the ground and shuddered. She must have made a noise.

"Let me take care of that," Vi said before she took off to make her magical preparations. She muttered something that Em couldn't understand and pointed her magically glowing hands at the scarily large pool of blood. At first, nothing happened, and then it seemed to shrink in on itself until there was nothing left.

Not even a stain on the light-colored carpet.

That was almost more impressive than whatever magic was powering the shadow beast. Em, at least, could see a use for something like that. It looked like it would beat vacuuming any day.

"Will you two be okay if I leave you alone?" Vi asked with a concerned look on her face.

Em should probably feel exhausted, but her body was thrumming with energy and she had Andre by her side. She wouldn't be alone at all. She nodded. "We're going to be fine."

Andre sucked in a deep breath and didn't say anything. She placed her hand on his leg, grounding him in her presence to tell him that she would be okay.

She hoped.

Vi left them alone, and it only took another minute for reality to crash down on her.

"Holy shit." She was a werewolf. She had almost died. And if it wasn't for Andre, she would have. "You saved my life."

"That's my job." He nuzzled his head against her, and Em knew for certain that he wasn't doing anything just because it was his job.

But she couldn't stand on the assumption anymore. "Why are you here?"

"You know why," he said, like it was the easiest thing in the world. "You hired me."

She didn't want that explanation. It wasn't enough. "Now is not the time for games, Andre."

He wrapped his arms tight around her. "I couldn't walk away if I wanted to. And I don't want to. You're my mate."

Mate. That word had been hovering around the outside of their interactions for more than a week now. Em knew it was the truth deep in her bones. It changed nothing between them. Everything she felt came from deep in her heart, and she didn't need faith to add some kind of extra layer to make it right.

She reached a hand up and cupped Andre's cheek, but she tried to pull back as she realized she was smearing her own blood against him.

Andre reached up and caught her hand. "I'm not afraid of it."

"We don't need this reminder." She didn't want to come to him covered in her own blood. She was fine now, but only barely. And she needed him to know things were going to be okay.

They got up and Em led him to the bathroom, where they both stripped off their clothes and she turned on the water of the shower.

The shower in the master bathroom of their suite was something that pornographic fantasies were made of, but for the first several minutes, as they stood under the water and let the blood wash away, thoughts of porn and sex and anything else were far from Em's mind.

And then she started to feel clean, and dirty thoughts intruded.

No. Not intruded.

She welcomed them in.

She ran soapy hands over Andre's fit body, her fingers tracing over the defined lines of his muscles and taking joy as he shuddered against her. If she looked lower, she would see his cock plumping up, and her mouth watered at the thought.

She pivoted them around so Andre was standing directly under the water, and she was a bit out of the spray when she dropped down to her knees, heedless of the tile floor. The warmth of the water somehow seemed to shield the hardness of the tile.

"Em…" Whatever he was going to say was cut off when she licked a broad swipe across his cock. He groaned and reached out a hand to steady himself while his other hand seemed magnetically attracted to her head. He rested it carefully on her hair, not forcing her to do anything, but not pushing her away. She wanted his fingers clutching her with careless abandon, and as she licked him again, she knew he was getting close.

He was already hard. And she felt powerful where she was, feeling the way his body responded to her and tasting the clean, masculine flavor of his flesh.

She took him into her mouth and sucked, and finally Andre's fingers dug into her hair and held on for dear life. If she could have smiled around his cock, she would have. But she turned her attention to giving him all of the pleasure that he had given her and then some.

It wasn't a competition. Not exactly.

But she still wanted to win.

Andre thrust against her, and if she hadn't expected it, she would've gagged. She couldn't exactly call herself an expert at giving head, but when it came to Andre, she was going to become a freaking professional.

And that's when she remembered she had hands and used them to help, stroking where her mouth couldn't reach and giving him the pressure that he needed.

He gasped out her name, and it might have been a prayer.

Her body was on fire with desire, even though she hadn't touched herself at all. She would've reached down to stroke her wet sex, but she was a bit concerned that the slippery tile of the floor would see her sliding off of her knees and down onto her ass.

Not exactly sexy.

She sucked even harder, and she was sure she had

Andre on the edge. The hoarse cries coming from his mouth got even more desperate as did the way he thrust against her.

But the man had more self-control than he should have and pulled away with an almost pained gasp.

"It's my turn."

34

ANDRE WAS on the edge of coming, and if he didn't take control of the situation, it would be over before it began. If they had all night, he would've reveled in the pleasure, knowing he had time to recover to bring his mate to the heights of desire over and over again.

But they didn't have all night. A plan was afoot, and these were stolen moments before danger came their way.

He shut the water off and helped Em to her feet.

Her lips were swollen, and he couldn't stop himself from kissing her. Why would he? It was everything he wanted in this world.

He backed her up against the shower wall and pressed his body flat against hers. Their lips moved together, and his body thrust against her stomach. It wasn't enough pressure. But it was close. And if he wasn't careful, he was still in danger of coming.

Andre tore himself away again. The room was cooling fast despite the heat of the shower, and he didn't want his mate shivering with cold. Not when she should be shivering with pleasure. They stepped out of the sumptuous shower and he handed her a towel and took one for himself. But she barely had it wrapped around herself before he swept her off of her feet and walked her to the gigantic bed they were sharing.

There was still a faint hint of blood in the room, despite Vi's magic. But the clean scent of soap was starting to overpower it, along with the scent of his mate.

Andre growled in pleasure. This was what it was meant to be.

He set Em down on the bed and her towel flipped open, revealing her naked form to him.

Yes. This.

Her body wasn't changed by becoming a werewolf, though the wounds inflicted by the shadow beast were nothing more than the faintest scars. Andre knelt between her legs and ran his lips over those scars, trying to take away the memory of the pain.

It wasn't enough. Nothing would ever be enough. He had failed in keeping her safe.

And as if his mate sensed the direction of his thoughts, she ran her fingers through his hair and tugged him up so that she could kiss him.

Kissing her was a pleasure unto itself. He could lose himself in the feel of their lips pressed together and never want for more.

At least, not until he thought about his cock and the feel of her tight heat wrapped around him.

"I'm your mate," Em said between kisses.

Andre just groaned.

"Make it real." It was a demand.

It was one that Andre wanted to obey more than he wanted to breathe. But something still made him ask. "Are you sure?" They didn't really know the repercussions. It was also new.

"Bite me before I bite you," was her threat and a promise, her eyes glowing with wolfish magic.

"I will," he said. But not quite yet. Not till they were completely joined together.

Andre reached down and found the apex of Em's sex already wet and ready for him. He prepared her, his fingers delving inside as he heard her moans.

And then he was sliding into her, his mind blanking in pleasure as her tight heat engulfed him.

Was this what it meant to be mated? This kind of joining that somehow felt closer than anything he'd ever experienced in his life?

Andre didn't know. But he was certain that Em

was it for him. No matter what happened, she was his mate just as he was hers, and there was no turning back from that.

He began to move and she moved with him, her fingers clutching tightly, now strong enough to leave bruises. She was stronger as a werewolf and she would learn to control that strength as time went on, but he would gladly wear her marks wherever she wanted to leave them.

He could feel his teeth getting sharper. He didn't know how it worked, or why he could summon things while in his human form when he couldn't do it at any other time.

Now was not the time to question things.

As he plunged deep inside of her and she began to ripple around him, he sank his teeth into her neck and left his Mark. He tasted her blood, but only for a minute before pulling away.

And when he pulled away, he was shocked to feel Em's teeth brushing against him, and she returned the favor and bit into his neck, marking him for herself.

It pushed Andre over the edge and he emptied himself inside of her.

They collapsed back onto the bed, spent and marked from their lovemaking.

Andre could barely string two thoughts together,

so he was surprised when Em spoke. "Do you think Vi's plan is going to work?"

He didn't know. But he refused to let doubt dampen the mood. "It has to work. It's the only way I get forever with you."

35

"It's going to work, I promise," Vi said with the kind of confidence that Em wanted to believe in.

But her hands were shaking as she clutched the two vials that Vi had prepared. She still couldn't quite wrap her mind around everything that had happened. She thought she had experienced eventful days before. They had nothing on *this*.

She wanted to run her fingers over the scar on her throat and take comfort in what it meant, but the vials in her hands prevented that. It didn't matter. She still knew the scar was there.

Claimed.

Mate.

Andre was just out of her sight, but she could sense him, smell him, feel him inside her heart. It was going to take some adjusting, but the best kind. Em didn't know how to have a partner, but when it came to Andre, she was happy to figure it out. And she got the feeling he was right there with her.

"Why couldn't we do this before?" she asked. The wolf had been stalking her for nearly two weeks. And Vi had known about the issue for over a week. She had a plan now. But Em was a little bit confused about the timing. Em's newly formed wolf was prowling under her skin and desperate to take action.

Vi pursed her lips and cast her eyes skyward for a moment. Whatever it was, she didn't want to say it.

"Spit it out," Andre demanded. He stood behind her, and his authoritative tone made her shiver. But there would be time for that later.

Vi heaved a huge sigh. "I'm not sure that Em would've survived if she was completely human."

Andre growled and charged at Vi, ready to pounce.

But the witch did a bit of magic and the air thickened in front of her. Andre ran into it like it was a wall. Em reached out and placed a hand on Andre's back to balance him.

"Explain." Em wasn't angry, not yet. But she had a feeling Andre needed to hear this.

Vi stared at Andre for several seconds, a challenging look on her face. She quirked up an eyebrow. He nodded. She let the magic fall and he didn't charge anymore. "We saw what the beast could do to you. When it wasn't being violent towards you, I thought we had time. But things have escalated now. And now you should be strong enough to withstand the spell and any potential attack."

"I thought you said it wouldn't attack this time." Andre vibrated with angry energy.

"I said it *shouldn't*." She put extra emphasis on the word. "This is all new to me too. Have faith. Another couple hours, and this will all be over."

Did Em have faith? She wasn't sure. But she definitely wanted it to be over, and Vi was their only option. "And you're certain that no one's going to be there?" They had taken time to study the layout of the hotel, and they had identified a spot to corner the beast. But Em didn't want to risk civilians.

Vi grimaced. "I can't risk putting up any magic to keep them away. That might tip off the beast. But I think we're good. I reserved the room for you to have a quiet meditation time. And I let the staff know that you're not to be disturbed. It's the best we can do."

"Why can't we just summon it back here to the hotel room?" It had attacked her once. She could still remember the feel of claws ripping into her.

"Because I think it got lucky the first time. It saw an opportunity and took it. And it's much more likely to run into people up here. Everyone's milling around since the concert was canceled." Vi's expression softened. "We don't have to do this today.

I can put the protections on your room like normal and we can find a better spot. Maybe outside. It's your call."

But if they didn't do this today, the wolf could attack again. And maybe it would begin to attack people that weren't just Em. Andre had already taken damage, and she didn't want him hurt again. And if this went right, they wouldn't have to worry anymore.

That settled it for Em. "Let's get this done."

She shoved one potion in her pocket and squeezed her hand around the second vial, grimacing as she got a whiff of it.

Vi scrunched up her nose in sympathy. "Sorry. I can't exactly add flavorings. Throws off the chemistry."

Em threw it back like a shot and wished she had a chaser. "Let's get this done."

She rushed across the hotel to the room that Vi had reserved; there wasn't much time before the potion took effect. It was a little bit out of the way, a small ballroom that would normally be used for corporate meetings or something like that. There were no tables in it right now and the lights were low. It would've been a good room for quiet meditation. But that wasn't why Em was there.

She started to feel something, the potion kicking in. It was supposed to make her a beacon for the shadow beast, to summon it towards her and pull it from whoever was in charge of its control.

Em felt exposed. Andre and Vi were nearby. If she concentrated on Andre, she could almost pinpoint him through their mate bond. But she had to focus on calling the shadow beast to her. It needed to get close.

She didn't want it to hurt her. She never wanted to feel pain like that again.

Her heart beat faster, and she was sure it was close. Who was controlling it? Why?

She would know soon enough. Or at least she hoped she would.

Em took a deep breath, and then she saw the wolf pad through the door.

It didn't charge at her quickly this time. It walked with a thoughtful pace, stalking halfway into the room and then pausing to look at her.

Did it know something was wrong? Was it capable of those kinds of thoughts?

Come on. Come on. She needed it to get closer. Vi had given her very specific instructions, and she couldn't do anything until the wolf was within touching distance.

The second potion was heavy in her pocket. Em's fingers were curled around it. She couldn't pull it out yet. She didn't know what the wolf would think, and she didn't want to give away that she had a trick up her sleeve.

The wolf took a few more steps towards her. But still not close enough.

Almost there. Em wanted to step towards it. But she didn't want it to spook and run away.

One more step. Then another. Then another.

It was almost there.

And then the wolf took a final step and it was close enough.

Em jerked the potion out of her pocket and threw the vial down onto the ground. The glass burst and a plume of red smoke billowed all around them.

The shadow beast howled as the potion surrounded it.

The howl grew louder and then cut off abruptly, leaving her ears ringing.

That was it then. The beast was gone.

But the smoke wasn't gone. And once it had dissolved the beast, the smoke billowed her way.

Vi hadn't said anything about this.

Em waved at it like she was trying to wave away campfire smoke, but that did nothing.

And then she was breathing it in. It burned. Her lungs ached as she swallowed it down, but there was nothing she could do to avoid it. She sucked it all down, and once there was not any red smoke left, she collapsed to the floor.

36

———

ANDRE COULD FEEL the moment something changed within Em through their mate bond. He and Vi burst through the door to the small ballroom to find Em climbing to her feet, her hands shaking a bit and her eyes glowing an impossible blue. "I know where he is." She swept by them and down the hallway.

Andre and Vi followed her. The shadow beast was nowhere to be seen, but that was to be expected. If Vi's magic had worked as it should, then the beast would be gone.

But what had the magic done to Em?

There was a concern at the back of Andre's mind, but he didn't have time to follow it up. Once this was done, once the witch was taken care of, he would figure out what Em needed and give it to her.

But not now. Not yet.

There were plenty of crew hanging around the hotel, and some of them must have seen Em. It would give lie to the story that Andre and Vi had spread around about her suffering from food poisoning. But that was another issue for tomorrow.

Em was moving fast, almost inhumanly so. And Andre and Vi had to run to keep up with her.

She turned another corner and stopped in front of the door, waving her hands in front of her until the door flew open as if a giant gust of wind had hit it.

That was new.

And it didn't have anything to do with being a werewolf.

"There!" Em pointed in the room.

Vi went in first. They were dealing with a witch, so it was a witch who needed to face the problem. But there wasn't much of a problem to face.

One of the musicians from Em's band was slumped over next to a small table with two candles and a piece of clothing that Andre would've bet a hundred dollars belonged to Em.

He looked at the man for a moment. "I thought witches were women," Andre said.

Vi gave him a strange look and a faint shake of her head. "Don't be sexist."

Was it sexist? It didn't matter. Andre just filed away the information in his head. Men could be witches too. He could feel his wolf stalking under his skin, demanding that he shift and rip the man's throat out.

"Jerry?" Em took two steps into the room, but didn't get within touching distance of the musician. "He seemed so nice."

"Apparently he was obsessed with you." Vi picked up a small diary that had fallen to the floor and started paging through it. There were cutouts of newspaper articles and magazine photos of Em. There were drawings and notes and plenty of information to show just how obsessed Jerry had been.

Andre's wolf growled, and he had to flex every muscle in his body to keep from shifting. The man was unconscious. He was out of the fight. And Andre wasn't going to hurt somebody who was already down.

"What do we do with him?" They couldn't exactly call the cops. The diary was disconcerting, but not illegal. And they couldn't really explain that Jerry had used magic to summon a shadow beast to attack Em.

But Vi was already kneeling down beside the man, her hands glowing as she waved them over him. "Witches have ways of dealing with people who abuse their powers," she said. "I will have someone come and take care of him." She turned to Em. "He won't bother you anymore."

Em closed her eyes and nodded, and her shoulders sagged as if all of the tension had finally left her body.

Andre stepped close to catch her if she was about to fall. He couldn't resist touching her and placed an arm around her shoulders. His skin prickled where it touched hers. It had never done that before, and he didn't think it had anything to do with the mate bond.

"You used magic," he said, and he wasn't talking to Vi. "I saw you open the door." It frightened him a little, but he wasn't scared of Em. He was scared for her. He knew how disconcerting it was to have a change like that thrust upon him, and he didn't want her to suffer.

Em shook her head from side to side, but she didn't say anything. She seemed exhausted, and Andre wanted to take her back to their room and watch over her while she slept.

"Did you do this to her?" It came out harsher than intended, but Em had been through enough, and Andre would do what he needed to do to protect her.

"Did I do what?" Vi challenged, eyebrows raised and fingers splayed, as if she was ready to defend herself with her magic. "Did I give her magic powers? Did I make her into a witch? No." She turned to Em. "What happened?"

Em took a few steadying breaths. "Can we talk in

another room? I… Looking at him… It's just—" She couldn't get the words out.

Andre backed her out of the room without another word, and Vi left a moment later, doing more magic to ensure that Jerry could not get free.

"Go up to your room," Vi told them. "I'm going to make a call and then I'll join you. We'll see if we can figure the rest of this out."

It felt like shirking his duty to trust Vi to see Jerry taken away. But the witch had been nothing but trustworthy thus far, and Em needed him more. Besides, Andre didn't exactly have someone he could call. As far as he knew, Gibson wasn't running a secret prison for magical creatures.

"I'll have them send you a text when he's in custody. They'll have a picture and everything," Vi offered while Andre hesitated.

It was good enough. Andre nodded and shepherded Em back to their room. She sat on the couch and didn't look back towards the bedroom. Andre couldn't sense any tension in her from the memory of what had happened earlier, but he stayed close to her, just in case.

Comfort went both ways, and the relief that his mate might finally be safe made him weak.

It was about fifteen minutes before Vi made it back. Andre's phone buzzed, and he had a picture of

Jerry tied up in very thick chains, sitting in what looked to be the back of a cake delivery van.

Did witches have secret prisons? Andre didn't know, and at the moment, he didn't care.

He and Em hadn't said a word to one another since getting back. They had just sat on the couch and he had held her as she tried to get her breathing under control.

When Vi got there, she let herself in and took a seat at the kitchenette table.

"What happened?" she asked, wasting no time with niceties.

And this time, Em was more ready to talk. "I threw the second vial down when it got close enough. And there was a lot of red smoke and it seemed to dissolve the beast. And then I breathed in all the smoke. I didn't want to. But I couldn't get away from it. What did it do to me?" Her eyes pleaded with Vi for answers.

Vi's face was grave, and she nodded once. "I'm sorry I didn't tell you about that possibility. That potion was attracted to magic. That's why it wanted you to inhale it. It might have been strong enough to awaken any sort of latent power you have. Or it will all go away in a couple weeks. Just be careful. Don't try and explode anyone with your mind."

Andre was too tired to be angry that Vi had kept that possibility from them. He doubted it would have changed anything, and he was starting to learn that Vi only gave information out in bits and pieces.

"I could do that?" Em sounded both excited and terrified at the prospect.

That broke Vi's grave expression, and even Andre smiled. "I've got a couple ideas," he said.

"Please refrain," Vi interrupted before they could start planning anything. "I'll give you a couple websites to go to. But if things don't look to be regulating within two weeks, give me a call. We may need to figure something out."

"Could I be both a werewolf and a witch?" Em asked. "Oh my God. What has my life come to?"

Andre tightened his grip on her. He wasn't sure if she was about to laugh or cry. Hell, he wasn't too far behind himself. This was fucking absurd.

But Vi didn't seem to find it strange. "I don't see why not. There's nothing incompatible with those two magics."

"What do you know about werewolves?" Andre finally asked. Now that they were safe, he needed to know. His *pack* needed to know. And Vi might be their only hope.

But she gave him a withering look and a disappointing response. "More than you, clearly. But that's a conversation for another day. We'll talk."

Then Vi got up and left them alone.

There was a lot more to know. But Andre felt

closer to the prospect of knowledge that he had in more than two years. At the moment, he didn't care.

He had his mate beside him, and it was time to convince her that everything was going to be all right.

EM ENDED up passing out shortly after Vi left her and Andre alone. And it was a miracle that she slept through the night. The next morning, she woke up, and for a second she thought it was all a dream. A very weird, terrible, and sometimes wonderful dream. Andre wasn't beside her. She couldn't hear him or smell him.

And then she heard something clank in the kitchen, and the knot in her chest loosened. Andre was out there. It had all happened. It was real.

She was a werewolf.

And maybe a witch.

And the shadow beast was gone.

Em sank back into the sheets and tried to breathe easy. Everything was going to be okay. It had to be.

Before she could get up, the door was opening,

and Andre had a tray full of food that smelled delicious. The man was a gift from heaven.

He set it on the bed beside her. "I thought you would be hungry," he said, leaning down to kiss her good morning.

"I could get used to this." It came out without thinking. But would she have time to?

She reached up and ran her fingers over the scar that had formed over their mating bite. It was a reminder of everything she and Andre could be together. But she belonged on the tour. And he had a life back in New York.

What was a brand new relationship compared to all that, even if fate had a hand in creating it?

She couldn't leave the tour. She couldn't leave her life. And she couldn't expect him to do the same.

Andre settled onto the bed beside her. "What's got that look on your face?" he asked gently.

Em reached for a piece of toast and nibbled on it to keep from saying anything. But that only stalled her for a moment. She considered eating something else, but it would become pretty obvious what she was doing. She was hungry, but not ravenous. "What happens now?"

Andre sucked in a ragged breath. "I don't know," he admitted with the kind of heartfelt honesty she wished he didn't have for the moment. She could have used a comforting lie.

Andre leaned in close, cupped her cheek, and kissed her gently. "It's going to take some figuring out. But I'm not about to leave you alone." He stayed close as he spoke, sitting on the bed next to her, careful to avoid the breakfast tray.

And the last of the tension left her. "What about your job?"

"We'll figure something out." He kissed her again. "Just because I was made into a werewolf with the rest of the pack doesn't mean that I need to be working for the company forever, too. We're still a pack. And you're part of that now. Maybe I'll cut back my hours. Maybe I'll take jobs when you're not on tour. Maybe the two of us will figure something else out. But I'm not letting this go. I'm not letting you go."

"I love you." It was fast. Faster than Em had ever fallen before. But this whole thing was unlike anything she had ever felt before. Andre was it for her. She had the bite mark to prove it.

And now it was his turn to grin. "You would kill me if I said I know right now, wouldn't you?" he asked, his grin getting even broader.

"Try it," but she was laughing.

"I love you," and then he covered her lips with his own.

Em shifted, slinging her leg on top of him to get into a better position, and that almost had the food spilling all over the sheets. She froze, half perched on Andre's lap as she considered her next move.

He made the decision easy when he reached around her and shifted the tray so it was balanced on the bedside table. It wouldn't take much to knock it to the floor, but Em found she didn't care. Not if it meant she got to keep kissing her mate.

She wasn't wearing much. She'd managed to throw on a ratty t-shirt before collapsing into bed the night before, but that was it. Andre, on the other hand, seemed to have gotten ready for the day for some strange reason.

She was going to fix that. She pulled at the fabric of his shirt until it was up and over his head and pitched to the other side of the room, exposing his naked chest. Much, much better.

"No more clothes for you," she said, raining kisses down on his collarbone and running her fingers over his naked skin.

A laugh rumbled out of him. "Is that rule for both of us?" he asked as he took the choice away from her and stripped her shirt off, leaving her naked.

With another person, she might have felt exposed, but never with Andre. His eyes on her were a blessing, one she never wanted to let go of. But she couldn't resist teasing him. "I make the rules here, buddy. You're my bodyguard, you have to do what I say."

She wasn't sure how he'd react to that, and she didn't expect him to flip their positions so she ended up flat on her back with Andre over her. It startled a yelp out of her, and she couldn't stop smiling. This was what happiness and relief were.

She was never letting him go.

He stripped off the rest of his clothes, and Em found she didn't mind her new position at all.

This man was her mate. What had seemed impossible at first now settled over her with the kind of certainty she'd never thought she'd have. Her career was too chaotic for relationships, she'd once told herself. Adding in magic and werewolves and all of that should have made it even worse.

But Andre was standing by her through it all. And she couldn't ask for more.

Andre's eyes seemed to waver between human blue and wolfish yellow as his wolf rose to the surface. Her own wolf seemed satisfied in her skin, happy to sit back and let Em take control. She crooked a finger, summoning her mate forward.

He was naked and hard, and as her eyes raked over him, her body lit up with the thought that he was all hers.

He loomed over her and they kissed again. She loved kissing him. He took control in a way that made her feel cherished, but the control was never too much. He seemed to understand her body in a way no one ever had before, and she didn't know if that came from their bond or if it was some special talent that was simply Andre.

At this point, she didn't care so long as he kept kissing her.

But she wanted more than kisses. She wanted everything. His lips. His cock. His heart.

A whole lifetime together.

And she was starting to believe it might be hers for the taking.

She shifted her weight and sent him rolling to the side, shocked a bit at the burst of power she hadn't expected. "Sorry," she muttered against his lips, kissing him again. "Unexpected werewolf powers."

Andre just smiled against her lips and kissed her harder as she lay on top of him.

She could feel his cock teasing her, and from this position she was the one in control. Not that she exactly felt in control of her body when lust was driving her like this. It was like she was possessed by the need for pleasure and unable to break free from its grip.

But why would she want to?

She positioned herself and felt the blunt head of his cock tease her entrance, and as she lowered herself over him, their eyes locked. And as she began to move, her heart sped up, and she was sure her own eyes bled to whatever their wolfish color was as something wild in her took over.

Andre reached out and laced their fingers together, another point of undeniable connection that anchored her heart and her body to his. He was impossibly hard within her, and still she wanted more. She sped up and her mate moved with her, their bodies joined in something timeless as pleasure arced between them.

And soon it was too much and Em broke, pleasure cresting through her as she came, shuddering around her mate. A moment later, he joined her, calling out her name with a final thrust as he came.

Sated and spent, she collapsed beside him and cuddled close. The soft words had already been said, and her body was too satisfied to do much else.

And then her stomach growled.

The triggered a laugh in both of them.

"Maybe it's time for breakfast," she admitted, reaching for the tray that had somehow managed to stay balanced on the table.

After another week and a half on tour, Andre and Em had managed to sneak in a three day break, and it was the first time they were heading back to see the pack. Gibson had called them all out to the farm in Pennsylvania, and the house was starting to feel more than a little crowded.

"How long do you think it'll be before he starts building a second cottage?" Owen asked him. He and Stasia had arrived only a few minutes after Andre and Em. Em and Stasia had immediately gone off to catch up, leaving him and his friend alone.

"You think we're getting a cottage? We'd be lucky enough if he built us barracks." Andre shuddered. That was definitely not something he missed about military life.

Owen gave him a playful shove as they headed

into the house. "Did you know Andre could smile?" Vega asked Jackson as he and Owen settled in.

Andre glared. The kid still hadn't made up for what he had done to Stasia several months before, and judging by the smile that had been knocked off of Owen's face, Owen hadn't forgotten either.

The kid put his hands up. "Sorry. Sorry." He took a few steps back, as if he expected Andre to lash out.

Andre had to bite back a grin. It was good to know that he could still scare the youngsters.

But before he could celebrate too much, Gibson called him and Rowe back to his office.

Rowe might not have been there to deal with the shadow beast, but he had been Andre's backup and Andre had been sending him updates since the very beginning. And with Andre now preoccupied with Em, it was Rowe who would be taking on most of the assignments.

He and Rowe sat in the guest chairs opposite Gibson's desk, and Gibson ignored his own chair to sit on the edge of the desk. "Have you had any more trouble since the witch helped you out?" He managed to say that all with a straight face, and if he had been anyone else, Andre might've congratulated him on that.

But he didn't have a death wish.

"No issues," Andre confirmed. Maybe he should have told Gibson and Rowe about the magic that Em had inhaled. Neither of them were sure exactly what it meant, but it wasn't his secret to tell. And he owed his loyalty to his mate. She could tell them if she wanted.

"Witches…" Rowe shook his head as he said it.

"Is that really so hard to believe?" Gibson asked. "After all, it was magic that made us what we are."

That night wasn't one Andre liked to remember. It was all hazy, but he remembered smoke and chanting and pain.

And then confusion. Confusion that was only amplified when he and the others were essentially kicked out of the military with what amounted to a giant payoff to buy their silence.

At first, Andre had thought they were trying to avoid an international incident. But weeks later, when they all changed into werewolves, he had wondered if the government knew what was coming.

"To be honest, I don't know what to think," Rowe admitted, steepling his fingers together. "One crazy wizard man, sure. But witches who are just regular people? Like accountants? That's weird."

"What do accountants have to do with anything?" Andre failed to see the connection.

Rowe rolled his eyes. "Nothing. I'm just saying that, like, accountants are normal and could be anyone. And apparently so are witches." Apparently, this made sense in Rowe's head.

Andre just stared at him.

So did Gibson.

Rowe slouched back in his seat, his point failing to land.

"Has the witch contacted you again?" Gibson asked.

"Not yet," said Andre. "But she said to give it a couple weeks." They needed Vi's knowledge, and Andre wasn't sure what Gibson would do if she didn't give it willingly.

"I want you on this, Rowe. This is a real lead. And maybe she can't get us information on who made us or why. But maybe she can give us more information on *what* we are. We need to know about witches. Are they friend? Foe? What other kind of mythological creatures exist? And we need to be subtle. They might not want to part with the information."

Vi had been happy to tell him and Em everything they wanted to know, but she had kept plenty to herself. At the end of the day, they had been more concerned about the shadow beast than anything else. And when he thought about it, Vi hadn't told him much outside of that.

Maybe she was keeping secrets. And maybe he had been too focused on keeping Em safe to notice.

But he couldn't regret that. She was safe now. And she was his.

What more could he want?

39

Stasia led Em to a small clearing at the edge of the nearby woods that must have been used by the pack. There were chairs set up all around the fire pit, and Em could just imagine how fun it would be to roast s'mores on a cool night. But the sun was high overhead, and she and her sister weren't out here for snacks.

Though Em could have used one. The drive out to the farm was long, and she had found that her werewolf metabolism had her eating a lot more. Oh well. She could suffer for a little while.

"Dad's talking with divorce lawyers," Stasia said as she settled into her seat. "I swear AR did a little dance when he heard that." AR was their oldest brother and their father's right-hand man.

Em felt just a little satisfaction at the news.

"Serves the name stealer right," she grumbled. Her father's wife, Riley, was technically her stepmother. She was also four years younger than Em. And when she had given birth to their father's tenth child, she had somehow managed to give Em's youngest sister the same name as Em: Emerald Selby. And then when Em pointed it out, she refused to change the kid's name.

Rude.

"Are you ever going to get over that?" Stasia asked with a grin. Em knew that her grumbling just amused Stasia.

She didn't care, it was the principle of the thing. "Is it really so much to ask that none of my siblings have the same name as I do? Is it really so much to ask that a woman that Dad marries *knows* all of our names? I don't think so."

Stasia tipped her head back and laughed.

After a moment Em joined her. "Okay. Maybe it's not such a big deal compared to... all of this." Werewolves. Magic. Mates. What was one name-stealing stepmother compared to that? Especially if she was soon to be an ex-stepmother. "I bet she gets screwed because the prenup."

"Do you feel bad for her at all?" Stasia actually seemed concerned.

That was cute. Em shrugged. "She had to know what she was getting into." That's what happened when a woman married a man nearly fifty years older than her.

Stasia didn't look so sure. "Dad is... Dad. If I didn't know better, I would say he could set spells on people. But he probably wouldn't have so many ex-wives if that's true."

Em didn't want to think about that. "Let's not think about Dad as a wizard." She could just imagine him in some ridiculous robe and hat. She shuddered. "Any other family updates?" she asked, desperate for a change of subject. Though Selby family updates could be horrifying in their own right.

Stasia shook her head. "I've been staying out of most of it. Just the normal nonsense."

Em knew exactly what she meant. Their father was the third richest man in New York. With that came a lot of bullshit, and Stasia had dedicated most of her life to trying to keep as far away as possible. Em couldn't blame her. It was one of the reasons she loved going on world tours so much. It was the perfect excuse not to visit home.

"Speaking of bigger things..." Em splayed her hands out in front of her.

"Oh my god, you're pregnant." Stasia's eyes were wide, and Em imagined her sister holding a baby.

"What? No!" Em put a hand over her stomach, as if she was defending it from invaders. And she was glad Andre wasn't here to hear the suggestion, if only so he didn't hear her horrified rejection. "Things are still new between Andre and me. We haven't talked about kids yet. That's a later thing. Much later." She wanted kids. Eventually.

Very, very eventually.

Not less than two months into her relationship and werewolfdom.

"Okay, so what bigger thing?" Stasia slumped, clearly not as excited by whatever Em was about to say.

And that got her to thinking. "You're not pregnant, are you?" Now she had babies on the brain.

Stasia's eyes got wide and she shook her head, not quite as startled as Em, but clearly not ready to consider it. "No. Let's make a pact not to talk about that for like a year. Or a decade."

"So no babies for you?" It had never been something she and her sister had discussed before. Neither of them had ever been serious enough about someone to really think about it. And now Em was with her forever guy, and it was crazy to think about how things could just fall into place like that.

"We want to figure out the werewolf thing first," said Stasia sensibly. "Will our kids be werewolves? Will we have to bite them if we want them to be wolves? Do we want that? There's so many questions. One thing at a time."

And that Em could understand.

She held out her hands again. "I've learned a couple tricks." She had to close her eyes and concentrate hard, but she could feel the energy swirling all around them and summoned it to her fingers. They lit up like Fourth of July sparklers, and she waved them around in front of her.

"What?" Stasia's mouth hung open in shock.

"So I might have accidentally inhaled the ghost werewolf that was stalking me and now I have magic powers. Maybe." It didn't sound any less crazy, no matter how many times she said it.

At that, Stasia blinked. "What?"

Em wished she had another trick to show, but all she had managed so far was the finger sparklers. It looked fun, but it wasn't exactly useful. Andre had been willing to be her guinea pig to see if they actually hurt, but when she touched his skin, he said they just tickled. Not exactly a weapon.

"I'm going to give Vi, the witch that helped us, a call pretty soon. She said the powers might dissipate, but so far nothing's changed. I don't know if I have enough power to be a witch or if I'm going to learn a few cool tricks. But apparently that's the thing now." She didn't know when she would have time to figure out these new powers. The tour still had months left on it, and she'd be going into the studio to record a new album soon enough. Her life was busyness on top of busyness on top of busyness on top of werewolf bullshit. And apparently, she would have to add witch crap to that as well.

"Maybe we should wait *two* years to talk about babies," was what Stasia finally said.

Em laughed. Two years was plenty far away. They could re-negotiate then. "You've got a deal."

40

THE SUN SET and Andre and Em were finally alone. The rest of the pack had already run off, but tonight it was just the two of them. He and his mate and miles and miles of safe land to run on. They had shifted before. But given that the tour took them from city to city to city, there wasn't much space where they could actually run.

City parks could be big, but they were also full of humans who knew nothing about werewolves and would be terrified if they spotted them.

"Are you ready?" Andre asked as he stripped off his robe and folded it nicely on the ground.

Em was still wearing her robe; she had it clutched tightly around herself. He knew it wasn't really modesty that was keeping her covered. And he wondered if she was suddenly afraid. And then she smiled and let her robe fall to the ground.

Her naked skin gleamed in the moonlight, and Andre the man and Andre the wolf fought for dominance to figure out what they wanted. He wanted to claim his mate again right there. A run could wait.

But she was already beginning to crouch down and breathe deep to bring on her shift.

"I'm going to win," she declared.

"Win what?" Andre knelt down beside her.

"Whatever there is to win. The prize is totally mine." She grinned and rubbed her hands together in anticipation.

Andre leaned in and kissed her. How could he do anything else?

"You're on." He was ready for a game.

They each let the change take them, and then they were off, racing deep into the woods as wolves. Together, just as they were meant to be.

Em raced ahead of him, and Andre sprinted to catch up. And when he overtook her, his mate sped up until they were both going as fast as they could.

It didn't last for long. They could only run so fast for so far, and the night was long.

But racing wasn't the only game that Em seemed intent to play.

And Andre wouldn't tell her, but no matter who

was the victor, he already had the greater prize. He had her. And he wasn't letting her go.

Andre leaned his head back and howled at the moon. A moment later, Em joined him.

And in the distance, they heard the pack join them as well.

It was everything Andre hadn't known to want. And then Em took off running again, and Andre chased after her.

This was life with his mate. And he couldn't wait to see what lay ahead.

WHEN EM INVITED Andre to the studio, he couldn't say no. She took the time specially even though they still had another few weeks of the tour, and she was using up one of her few free days to get the song in her head recorded.

She'd been working on it for a while. And every time he asked about it, she stuffed the little notebook she was working on away and refused to say a word.

At first, Andre had been a bit offended. But he realized he was just seeing her process. She didn't want to share anything until she was ready.

And now she was ready and she was sharing it with him.

They met the producer, and then Andre was directed to take a seat on the couch in the back. He didn't know exactly what was going to happen.

His knowledge of what went on in a music studio was contained mostly to VH1 specials and movies. But now this was the real thing. Em picked up a guitar and played a few chords for the producer, and after a few moments, they were ready to get to work.

And when she opened up her mouth, Andre was rapt.

She spoke of darkness, of the night, and the moon, and of magic. It was all metaphor to someone who didn't know what their lives were like.

But he was hearing the story of the two of them put into words for anyone to hear.

It was a love song. Their love song. And if Em didn't already own his entire heart, he would've given it to her in that minute.

Their eyes locked, and she looked at him through the soundproof glass. Andre pushed himself up from the couch and got closer so he could watch her sing.

After the chorus, she stopped and spoke to the producer again. And then she turned to him.

"What do you think?"

Andre just grinned. "I love it."

"It still needs some work."

"I can't wait to see what you do with it."

With his heart. With his life. Because they were together now and weaving their own kind of magic. And there was no going back.

And Andre couldn't wait to hear more of the music they would create.

Thank you for reading On the Prowl!
I'd appreciate it so much if you would consider leaving a review.

Can a man without emotions find his mate?

There's nothing left in Raze. No love, no hate, nothing but the duty that he owes his people. But when he meets a fascinating and tough human woman on a barren planet something deep inside comes back to life and for the first time in years he yearns for more.

Can she trust the ice cold warrior?

When a mission for the Sol Intelligence Agency gets out of hand, Sierra will need to use every skill she has and work with a mysterious alien warrior who awakens an unquenchable desire within her. He's cold and forbidding, but when he looks at her there's a fire in his eyes that opens up a whole world of possibilities.

Two worlds collide...

The chemistry between Raze and Sierra is too hot to ignore, even if it should be impossible for a mate bond to form between them. They'll need to fight pirates, their people, and fate itself to be together. But it may already be too late for the soulless warrior and the woman he aches to claim.

Download the ebook for free!

Also available in audio and paperback

Looking for something else? Kate Rudolph has a heart pounding collection or paranormal and sci-fi romance stories for you! Bundles, bears, audiobooks, aliens, and more. Check out your options in the list below. You can find out all you need to know at www.katerudolph.net.

Want to check out one of the books? Click on the series name to find out more!

Zulir Warrior Mates

Kidnapped humans. Alien Warriors. Electric wings.

The Zulir Warrior Mates series brings you human heroines and heroes abducted from Earth who find love – and wings! – with the alien warriors who rescue them.

Also available in audio!

Synnr's Saint

Synnr's Hope

Synnr's Spark

Synnr's Kiss

Guarded by the Shifter

Werewolf. Bodyguard. Mate.

The origins of these shifters are shrouded in mystery, but they're determined to protect their mates from any harm that comes their way.

Also available in audio!

Hunting Season

On the Prowl

Detyen Warriors

Detya was destroyed a hundred years ago. These doomed warriors are out to find justice… and their mates.

The Detyen Warriors series brings you kick butt heroines, alpha alien heroes, fated mates, and relationships strong enough to span the galaxy!

The entire series is also available in audio!

Soulless

Ruthless

Heartless

Faultless

Endless

Alien Holiday Romance

Christmas… in space????

These alien holiday romances look beyond Earth's winter holidays and ring in the season across the galaxy! *Select titles available in audio*.

Snowed in with the Alien Beast

The Alien's Winter Gift

The Alien Reindeer's Wild Ride

Trapped with her Alien Mate

Alien Outlaws

Outlaws, schemes, and love… it's all there in the Alien Outlaws series…

Andie Munster is sick of life on Ixilta, the planet she got dumped on after being abducted from Earth six years ago. And when the mysterious and dangerous Xandr shows up looking for a way off the planet, she's half-prisoner, half-co-conspirator in a wild rush to escape.

Rogue Alien's Escape

Rogue Alien's Woman

Rogue Alien's Secret

Rogue Alien's Legacy

Mated to the Alien

Fated Mate Alien Romance

Detyens are doomed to die young if they don't find their fated mates.

Follow along as these mated pairs fight off aliens, corrupt dictators, prejudiced humans, pirates, and more! The books can be read or listened to in any order, though some characters show up in multiple stories.

Select books available in audio.

Pick a book and jump into the action today!

Ruwen

Tyral

Stoan

Cyborg

Krayter

Kayleb

Shayn

Braxtyn

Doryan

Dekon

Stealing the Alpha

The thief takes what she wants, but the alpha keeps what's his...

Join shifter thief Mel as she clashes with lion alpha Luke in an explosive trilogy of two opposites who can't keep away from one another.

Also available in audio!

The Alpha Heist

Entangled with the Thief

In the Alpha's Bed

Save with box sets!

Aliens. Shifters. Warriors. Mates. Get them all wrapped together in these special box sets. Save up to 30% off the price of buying the individual books, depending on the series!

Alien Outlaws: The Complete Series

Mated to the Alien Volume One (also available in audio)

Mated to the Alien Volume Two (also available in audio)

Mated to the Alien Volume Three

Mated to the Alien Volume Four

Stealing the Alpha: The Complete Series (also available in audio)

The Mate Bundle

Detyen Warriors Volume One (also available in audio)

Detyen Warriors Volume Two (also available in audio)

Standalone Paranormal and Sci-Fi Romance:

Crashed

Mated on the Moon

Mated to the Alien Dragon

Marked

Bear in Mind

Alpha's Mercy

Gemma's Mate

Find more by Kate Rudolph at www.katerudolph.net

ABOUT KATE RUDOLPH

Kate Rudolph is a paranormal and alien romance author who lives in Indiana. She loves writing about kick butt heroines and the steamy heroes who love them. She's been devouring romance novels since she was too young to be reading them and had to hide her books so no one would take them away. She couldn't imagine a better job in this world than writing romances and sharing them with her fellow readers.

If you enjoyed this story, please consider leaving a review.

www.ingramcontent.com/pod-product-compliance
Lightning Source LLC
Chambersburg PA
CBHW021123190726
48288CB00008B/2474